THE PERFECT COUPLE

NJ CRACKNELL

BLOODHOUND
BOOKS

Copyright © 2024 NJ Cracknell

The right of NJ Cracknell to be identified as the Author of the Work has been asserted by him in accordance with the Copyright, Designs and Patents Act 1988.

First published in 2024 by Bloodhound Books.

Apart from any use permitted under UK copyright law, this publication may only be reproduced, stored, or transmitted, in any form, or by any means, with prior permission in writing of the publisher or, in the case of reprographic production, in accordance with the terms of licences issued by the Copyright Licensing Agency.
All characters in this publication are fictitious and any resemblance to real persons, living or dead, is purely coincidental.

www.bloodhoundbooks.com

Print ISBN: 978-1-916978-86-7

For my godchildren, with apologies.

If thou canst cuckold him,
Thou dost thyself a pleasure,
Me a sport.
— Iago, *Othello*, William Shakespeare

PROLOGUE

I've always wanted to live by the sea.
Ever since I was little and my mother used to take me to the beach at Lyme Regis and we'd get cones of chips and ice cream with 99s for after.

The smell of the fresh salty air, the cries of the seagulls warping gently in the wind, the smiles on people's faces as they splash about in the water, the hulls of the fishing boats as they sit lopsided at low tide, my mum lovingly applying the coconut lotion to my red shoulders after I spent too much time in the sun...

Yep, there's something undeniably magical about the sea. Especially since my father wasn't there.

When you are young you don't think about the obstacles that might arise when you are chasing your dreams. You just take it for granted that one day, with enough resolve and dedication, and if you want it enough, you will obtain everything that you deserve.

And as I look out at the stunning panoramic sea view from the rear deck of Coastguard's Cottage, I know I've obtained everything I deserve. Sure, there have been obstacles along the way, some considerably bigger than others, but nothing I couldn't handle. I'm a person who strongly believes in the power of desire. Desire drives some people more than others, and I've been driven very strongly by mine.

A cottage by the sea, with a couple of kids running around in the garden, maybe playing with a hose, and the knowledge that I got here off my own back, not letting anything or anyone get in my way? Yeah, I guess that's what I've always secretly wanted. And who cares that I don't have a partner to share it with? As the old saying goes, there are plenty more fish in the sea! And I live so very close to the sea now.

What's that? Do I regret some of the things I've had to do to land this little slice of heaven? Not really. Because it's what I deserve, you see? It was my destiny to end up here, in the delightful little town of Treme-on-Sea, in this amazing little cottage by the beach, with two precious kids running around and blossoming before my very eyes.

It's really something for a person to be able to say they have everything in life that they desire. How many people truly get to say that? I know there will be questions raised, judgements passed, suspicions aired, but I've covered my tracks well. So well that there's zero chance of any blowback. How could there be? All the loose ends have been tied up.

And if you had asked me, as that little kid playing on the beach all those years ago, 'Would you be willing to make the ultimate sacrifice to get what you want? Would you be willing to kill to get it?' I know exactly what my answer would have been.

You're damn right I would.

1

NEVIN

Buying an old house was always going to have its pitfalls. Buying an old and run-down former coastguard's cottage, on a weathering cliff, a literal stone's throw from the sea? Well, that's just a step or two short of folly. But when you have a wife like mine, you have to think outside the box in order to keep her happy.

Now, it wasn't as if we were *un*happy prior to this upheaval. Far from it. We lived in a modest semi on the outskirts of a beautiful Roman city in the south-west of England, with our own garden, plenty of parking and a core group of great friends. Our two young kids Amy and Josh were thriving at a nearby independent school and we had a decent chunk of cash in the bank, thanks to our combined careers going fairly well at this stage of our lives.

But my wife Gloria – and you have to respect a woman who knows what she wants – had always wanted to live by the sea. *It's just something about the air,* she loved to say. And I have to say, I absolutely agree. There's a great deal to be said for waking up in the morning with the salty tang of the ocean filtering in through the bedroom windows, then walking out barefoot onto a wooden deck and taking in a view most people would kill for, all while leisurely drinking your morning coffee.

Plus, since moving to Treme-on-Sea in the stunning coastal county of Devon my hayfever symptoms have all but disappeared. And that alone was almost enough to make the significant uprooting of our family worth it. That and getting my wife to stop her almost daily pleading that we get out of the city and closer to the beach. For the kids, of course.

It did mean a good deal of stress and hand-wringing while the sale of our semi went through and we waited for the mortgage to be approved on the cottage, but yes, in balance, I'd say it was worth it.

At first.

But as I said, when you take on an old property dating back to the 1850s, you don't just get period features and hominess. You also get damp, crumbling pointing and drainage issues because the iron pipes have not been replaced for 170 years. And 170 years of salt air is really not kind on iron. Not to mention the steep stone steps leading up to the front door. I'd warned the kids about those, picturing sprained or even broken limbs when the winter frosts arrive.

Also, the previous owner had done some work to bring the property into line with modern standards of living, but they'd cut every corner possible. So they'd connected the cottage to the main drainage system, but left the old septic tank, mostly empty, under the garage. Ageing septic tanks are pretty much top of the list of the crap you want to get sorted out because they are prone to collapsing. And of course, the Environment Agency takes an interest, and you're supposed to get someone with a licence to do the work, and that was only one of the things we've had to sort out since we moved in.

But I begrudgingly got on with it. I say begrudgingly, but I had decided to take a break from writing for the few weeks leading up to my birthday anyway. I was kind of glad of the distraction. There is after all only so much time you can spend hiking up and down coastal paths.

Also, drains? It's really a man's job isn't it? I know most women could easily deal with the problem just as well as a man, but when I'd mentioned to Gloria that she was more than welcome to don the elbow-length Marigolds and stick her arm into a septic tank, unsurprisingly she wrinkled her nose and told me to knock myself out. Plus she was busy migrating her business from city to coast, and that involved several trips a week back to our previous hometown to sort out the legalities.

Another great thing about our lives was that we were technically able to work from anywhere now. Me, as a writer of moderately successful political thriller novels, and Gloria as a literary agent who had a burgeoning number of clients across the UK, and now abroad as well.

No, before you ask, my wife was not *my* agent; something that did occasionally cause some tension between us. It wasn't because I didn't believe in her talents. I know a lot of book agents, and Gloria was practically the only one, bar my own, whose methods I respected. But as I was an established writer before Gloria's career change, I avoided the old 'don't crap where you eat' adage by continually remaining faithful to my own agent, who had been with me from the start of my writing career.

I'm standing outside the front of our dream cottage by the sea and watching as the cement lorry reverses very slowly up the cobbled driveway towards the garage. I feel pretty silly waving my arms at the driver, who studiously ignores my attempt at directing him, as if he needs instructions on how to do his job. The tail-lights flash and the truck emits that nauseating high-pitched beeping that they all seem to do when in reverse. It stops just inches short of the overhead door to the garage and the ruddy driver jumps out, sweating heavily in the late morning heat. He's over an hour late, but I'm too consumed in my own thoughts to give him any gyp for it. I just want this goddamn job out of the way so I can begin to *think* about relaxing after undoubtedly the most stressful week of my life.

'Where's it going then, mate?' he shouts over the truck radio, which he's refused to switch off along with the ignition. Aqua's 'Barbie Girl' plays just a little too loudly for my ears but I remain cool, knowing that in just a few minutes all my troubles will essentially be behind me.

I point at the manhole in the far corner of the garage. It's a two-foot circular hole in the solid concrete floor, underneath which lies the disused septic tank we are now filling in. I watch nervously as he grabs the hosing off the back of the truck and leads it up to the open hole. Satisfied it is safely in place, he waddles back to the rear end of the truck and presses a few buttons. Seconds later, liquid concrete gushes out of the hose and into the empty tank in the ground, gradually filling it forever.

Well, I *say* empty.

But for the bodies weighted down with chain at the very bottom of it.

2

NEVIN

ONE WEEK EARLIER

The marquee is erected, the bunting is up, and my daughter Amy is busy writing up the bar menu on the big chalkboard we had gotten her for her twelfth birthday. I am a week shy of my fortieth birthday party and preparations are in full swing.

The garden at the rear of the cottage is blooming nicely. It's the middle of May, and the chrysanthemums, peonies and other flowers are really starting to brighten up in the foreground. And then you look up and take in the stunning sea view out over the English Channel.

It never fails to take my breath away.

Our garden backs directly onto the path that runs the length of the entire Jurassic coastline, and every so often a group of hikers will emerge from view behind the hedge as they stroll along merrily, waving as they descend the steps down towards the beach at the southern tip of Treme-on-Sea. If you are ever out in the garden, and I am a lot, it's hard to stop yourself waving back and shouting a welcome to these seekers of leisure. Almost always they have smiles on their faces, and some are only too keen to stop and shoot the breeze for a few moments whilst they catch their breath.

There's just something about being close to the sea…

My son Josh appears at the open back door and shouts, 'Daaad! When's lunch?'

Like most eleven-year-olds he only ever wants to know two things: what time he is eating, and what football teams will be playing that evening when we sit down and watch a game together.

'There's cold turkey in the fridge,' I shout in reply. 'Make yourself a sandwich, big guy. Oh, and one for your sister. Extra mustard.' I wink at him.

He rolls his eyes in mock disgust at the thought of doing anything for his sister, then disappears back into the house.

'How's the menu coming along, sweetie?' I ask Amy, who is concentrating hard enough that her tongue is sticking out.

'Good! How do you spell mo-heet-oh?' she calls back.

I feel somewhat guilty entrusting a twelve-year-old with the job of writing up the various alcoholic cocktails we are going to be serving at the party, but she had insisted and Gloria had not given me that wilting look that seemed to suggest I was a terrible parent for allowing it, so it was all good.

'M.O.J.I.T.O.' I spell slowly, and Amy nods in a very grown-up way and goes back to her work. I notice with a flushing sense of pride and love that she is putting every effort into giving the chalkboard menu a Spanish theme. Given that is the theme of my party (not my choice, but a random one selected by both kids, and since it was the one thing they had ever agreed upon I had rolled with it), she has drawn various donkeys, cactuses, and, unusually, a mermaid in coloured chalk around the corners. I think about asking her how exactly a mermaid symbolises Mexico, but then think better of it.

She writes M and O before she stops abruptly and looks up

at me with questioning eyes. 'Did you say M.O. *J*? Where's the *djuh* in mojito?'

'It's Spanish, darling, they pronounce their Js as Hs.' I laugh, privately thinking that as she has been taking Spanish lessons at school for over three years she should really know that. Then I remember exactly how much Russian I remember even after reading it at university and instantly forgive her.

I survey the garden with a panoramic sweep of my eyes. I have to admit, it's starting to look very good. I was against the whole idea of a fortieth birthday party at first, having reached that stage of my life where I really didn't want to be celebrating getting older. But Gloria and the kids had insisted it was a milestone that had to be celebrated. I wonder if Gloria might think the same way in five years' time when she hits the Big Four Oh and has two teenage kids to watch around such a plentiful supply of booze.

We have invited around fifty people, variously made up of friends and business acquaintances. Alarmingly few from my line of work, and alarmingly many from Gloria's. But then my job basically entails sitting behind a desk for six hours a day in the little home studio I've carved out for myself in the garage, trying desperately to be the next Frederick Forsyth or Tom Clancy, whereas Gloria's involves travelling Europe schmoozing an endless list of clients and publishers. So it's only natural, I guess, that her numbers vastly outweigh mine in terms of the invitees.

It had been much the same at our wedding thirteen years before. The bride's side of the church was overflowing with Gloria's seemingly limitless family members, relatives and friends, whereas my side consisted of my parents, my best man Felix and a few old school buddies. I always thought that the older you got the fewer friends you ended up bothering with, but it seemed to be the opposite in Gloria's world.

Still, what's that they say about life beginning at forty? I don't know if that really rings true with me. I have pretty much everything I want out of life. A beautiful wife, two healthy and blooming kids, a decent if not spectacular income and a cottage by the sea. Did I mention the sea view?

What more could possibly 'begin' at forty? I was pretty much as content as I could be, without a million quid in the bank. All I need right now is for my wife to get back from her work trip to Liechtenstein (yes, you read that right) where she is trying to sign a hotly-tipped feminist author, and life will be damn near perfect.

Funny how things can change.

3

NEVIN

With the kids fed and getting ready for bed I stretch my weary legs and pour a large glass of red wine, before sitting down to tackle the seating plan for the party. Gloria had insisted she would take care of it, but as she is already doing pretty much everything else from hiring the marquee and the musicians to sourcing the food and drink, I think I'll get a head start and surprise her for when she gets back.

The sun is setting over the much smaller garden at the front of the cottage, and I decide to take my wine outside and enjoy the last of the day's warmth. As I rise, Josh comes running out of the bathroom, soaking wet and wrapped in a towel, complaining that the hot water has run out.

'I'm sorry, buddy. Looks like your sister's shower was a bit longer than she was planning.'

'It's not fair!' he shouts. 'She always gets in first and takes all the hot water!'

'Well, you'll just have to be super ready to get there first next time I shout ready for bed, eh?' I say gently. 'Tell you what, why don't I give you a heads-up tomorrow night and you can jump in before she does?'

I give him a crafty wink which seems to imply we are in cahoots in getting one up on his sister, which is always a good way to keep him happy. I don't like doing it, and know I will have to go through the exact same routine with Amy the next night in order to maintain balance. But it quells the uprising for now and he skulks off to the fridge to get yet another snack with goosebumps all over his shivering little body.

That reminds me there is yet another thing on my to-do list. Sort out a new boiler. The heating system in the cottage dates back to the 1950s, I think, when the last occupant took it over. It almost certainly hasn't been updated since. The storage tank is about the size of a pedal bin, and is woefully underequipped to provide a family of four, two of whom are pre-teens, with their daily supply of hot water.

But before I can get a new heating and water system installed, we have to get connected to the mains gas supply. This involves digging a trench down the drive and onto the public access way to hitch the house up to the system. The council has given us permission to do this but I was yet to find a contractor who would quote us anything less than a staggering twenty grand. And that was before we even bought the boiler and paid someone to fit a new central heating system.

I sit back down, quietly weighing up the pros and cons of the house move, as I do most nights. We have left the comfort and connectivity of a city pad behind to move back to the kind of post-war home 'comforts' our grandparents would have had to put up with. We're okay right now as summer is just starting, but I don't want to think about the kind of cold we will experience come the winter if we don't get the damn heating system sorted out before then.

And don't get me started on the wi-fi speed. Back in the city we enjoyed full fibre and speeds of over 500mbps per second. Gloria and I thought nothing of streaming Netflix while both the kids used their iPads in their rooms. Wanna know what the download speed is in Coastguard's Cottage, Treme-on-Sea?

A whacking great 1.5mbps.

I'd forgotten what it was like to try and send an email at dial-up speed. Gloria complained about it non-stop, albeit under her breath when she thought I couldn't hear, and always quickly switches to something like how great it is to be able to keep chickens in the garden when I'm back in earshot. I think she does it for my benefit as she knows how much I had been reluctant to uproot the family to the dark side of the M5 motorway.

In the front room I hear the kids break into their latest fight, which involves Josh holding a Rubik's cube the wrong way, so I usher them into their bedrooms and tell them they can have an extra half hour on their tablets before lights out. As always, this appeases them and they instantly go silent as they focus on their all-powerful screens.

I sigh and take my wine out into the front garden to watch the chickens peck around and enjoy the last of the daylight before they head into their coop for the night, no doubt to go about the business of laying us some fresh eggs for breakfast. All thoughts of the party seating plan have gone out of my head after the kids' fight, and I just need five minutes to calm down before I set my attention to anything other than relaxation.

I think about a crafty cigarette, but Gloria had said she would be back around 10pm and I know even with ninety minutes' grace she'll still be able to smell it on me. I ease myself into a hard patio chair (the cushions were lost in transit of course) and breathe in the sea air whilst focusing on being calm.

It is a balmy early summer evening. I can hear some sort of folk music floating up from The Green, the central space in the middle of town that frequently holds mini festivals at this time of year. I catch the smell of blooming flowers and instinctively breathe through my mouth to avoid a sudden attack of hay fever. Then I remember I have hardly suffered from it at all since the move and allow myself to take in the heady scent. Carefully. It's glorious.

Just then I hear a car coming up the gravel lane that leads up to our driveway. A taxi pulls up and Gloria shimmies out, collecting her overnight suitcase from the seat beside her. Crikey, she's home early! Good job I didn't sneak that cigarette.

She catches sight of me sitting in the front garden and throws me a wave and a smile, the one that makes her face light up like a firework display and used to make my stomach quiver. Her summer dress swings around her swaying hips as she walks up the driveway towards me. As ever I am struck by how incredibly feminine and beautiful she is. I rise to envelop her in my arms and she reaches up to kiss me, before wrinkling her nose and pulling back.

'Oh! Someone needs a shower...' she says lightly.

'Nice to see you too, honey,' I say, trying to kiss her again, but she has bent down to set her luggage on the patio. 'What are you doing back so early?'

'I managed to catch an earlier train. I would have texted but I wanted to surprise the kids! They are still up, aren't they?'

'They're having some quiet time,' I say sternly. 'There was an incident with a Rubik's cube.'

Gloria nods knowingly and makes for the house. She looks flustered. There is a light sheen of sweat over her chest that ten years ago would have made my shorts stir.

'I'll just go and kiss them goodnight then,' she says over her shoulder.

It's an odd way to greet me. I feel slightly uneasy as I sit waiting for her to return, which she does around five minutes later, carrying a cup of herbal tea.

'No wine?' I say. 'I would have thought you'd reach straight for the bottle after a journey like that. Speaking of which, how was the great nation of Liechtenstein?'

She was looking at me strangely. If I didn't know how to read her better I would almost say she looks... guilty.

'No wine tonight,' she says quietly. 'I've got some news, actually. I'm pregnant.'

4

NEVIN

Now this is not news I was expecting to hear. I spit out my wine all over my blue Ralph Lauren shirt.

'What?!' I choke. 'Well...' I couldn't think of anything better to say, so just repeat myself. 'What?'

Gloria takes a deckchair and eases down into it slowly, looking at me with a mixture of worry and humour. 'Yeah, I know. I'm pregnant, Nevin.'

To say this is a shock is an enormous understatement. For a number of reasons, which I'll come on to later. All I can do is stare in front of me feeling like a ton of bricks has landed on my head. My mind is racing, and I'm trying to think back to the last time we had sex. With the house move, organising the party and the general stresses that come with two pre-teen kids, I realise I can't remember.

'Well, aren't you going to say anything?' says Gloria after a number of seconds of silence.

'I'm sorry,' I say. 'I'm just trying to grip this in my head. You are?'

'Yep,' she says breezily. 'I realised I was late last week, so I took a test. To be sure, I went to the doctor just before I left for my trip. I'm up the duff.'

I'm partly astonished, and partly angry, but still mainly disbelieving. 'Before you left?! Well, why didn't you tell me?'

'I just needed a couple of days to get my head round it,' she says, as if it's the most normal thing in the world.

'I'm not bloody surprised!' I say, a little too loudly. I am aware that our nauseatingly nosy neighbours Chris and Lorraine are probably out in their garden and can hear everything we say, separated though we are by a large hedge and fence.

'Shh!' says Gloria under her breath. 'The last thing we need is them knowing.' She nods her head vigorously at the boundary to our respective houses.

Chris and Lorraine are decent enough people, or so we had come to believe, only having known them for a few weeks. But the few conversations I have been roped into over the hedge with Lorraine almost always feature her gossiping about the other residents of the lane. Bernard and Laura are getting an extension above their garage without planning permission and other crap like that.

We sit in silence for a few more seconds while we both come to terms with the knowledge that our lives are about to be disrupted even more.

Gloria is conspicuous in her silence. She usually would have been babbling about her trip and telling me all the ins and outs of the fabulous dinners and introductions she'd arranged to woo her new client. Now she just sits quietly, and is she *biting her lip?* I know that to be a sure sign of her nerves. And I'm not in the least bit surprised.

'How far along are you?' I say eventually, taking a large gulp of my wine.

'About seven weeks,' she says. 'It must have been that time after...'

'After Paul and Sarah's fortieth,' I interrupt, suddenly remembering the drunken fumble we'd had at our friends' joint birthday party in Gloucester. 'Fuck, I knew I should have packed a condom!'

The birth control conversation was not one we'd had for quite some time. Mainly because it had caused quite a few arguments early on in our relationship. Being the typical bloke I am, I couldn't understand why when we'd first started dating Gloria had refused to go on the pill. She had claimed it played havoc with her hormones and she'd never found the right brand to use. I'd relented and had worn protection myself ever since, apart from when we were trying for Amy and Josh, of course. But in the last couple of years our lovemaking had become so sporadic. And when we did make love it was more often than not completely spontaneous and after a few drinks. And let's face it, when you're not getting much, and you're drunk, you're just so happy to be getting laid that you often neglect the very important aspect of contraception.

There is another reason for my current state of disbelief as well though...

Come to think of it, Gloria does look a little nauseous. But she has just had a long trip.

'This is all a bit unexpected,' I say eventually. 'I mean, do you really want another baby? I'd kind of assumed we were past all that.'

I instantly regret *that* comment.

'Past it?' Speak for yourself, you old gammon!' Gloria says with irritation. 'I'm only thirty-five.'

'Yes but... do you really want to go through that all over again? The sleepless nights, the nappy changing, the endless mess...'

'No of course I don't!' she says a little too quickly. A tear wells up in the corner of her eye. 'I can't imagine worse timing, what with the house move and my business really taking off.'

'Well...' I say, grasping for the words. 'What do you want to do?'

'Why does it always have to be *my* decision?' she shouts. Chris and Lorraine will almost certainly know something is up now. Great, that's one goddamn conversation I am not looking forward to having.

'I'm sorry, that came out the wrong way,' I stutter, trying to get a grip on my emotions. 'I mean, what are *we* going to do?'

'I don't know,' she says defiantly. 'I can't make this decision now. I need to...'

She trails off, and I get the impression she was about to say 'talk to my mother'. And whoop-de-do, that's the one thing I was hoping she wouldn't say. Gloria's mother Susan can charm the tits off a cow but she can also be incredibly judgemental, and I know for a fact that she will be far from over the moon about another grandchild and the associated childcare obligations that said grandchild will entail for her.

Susan lives with her partner Robin in the next town along, which is part of the reason we chose to move to this area in the first place. I had to be one hundred per cent sure it was definitely the next town along and not Treme-on-Sea *itself* she lived in before I even considered the move in the first place. Susan is a part-time model and a full-time socialite, and she loves her space. So much so that I don't think she was entirely enamoured with us moving so close to her either.

I'm being mean. She's a doting grandmother and the kids absolutely adore her, but she is bit too airy-fairy for my liking and I'll admit I am more than a little concerned about the influence she might exert over my children.

'Of course, talk to your mum,' I say a little too abruptly, and before I can say anything else more soothing Gloria rises quickly from her deckchair and makes her way inside the house, digging her phone out of her purse as she goes. 'Could you bring my bag in please,' she says over her shoulder. 'Not now. In a while.'

I get the message.

I sit on the hard chair with my arse having gone numb going over the last five minutes.

Pregnant. *Jesus.* I am forty in a week and I assumed my days of getting up in the middle of the night to tend to a screaming infant were long behind me.

There is another reason I was more than a little anxious, though. What Gloria doesn't know, because I have never told her, is that I had a vasectomy three years ago.

That little baby growing in Gloria's womb could not have been put there by me.

5

GLORIA

Before you judge me, you should know a few things about my husband.

First off, Nevin is as charming a guy as you could ever hope to land. He's smart and erudite, with that infuriating ability to make everything he does seem easy. Okay, he may not have a face that could launch a thousand ships – maybe one or two yachts and a dinghy – but he has an inner confidence that makes him, I don't know... just stand out from the crowd.

That's the thing about men. A man can look like George Clooney and be worth all the money in the world, but if he lacks that underlying swagger, that aura of self-belief without it descending into arrogance, then he'll always find himself wanting with women. Confidence just seems to pique a woman's interest. Almost as if they want to find out where it came from in order to understand him just a little more. At least, that's how I've always felt about men.

Nevin has that in spades.

You know that feeling when you're in a crowded room and someone magnetic walks in and you just sense it? How everyone seems to take notice whether they want to or not? It's hard to describe but some men just have a... *quality*.

It helps that he's tall. Not too tall so as to attract unnecessary attention, but just tall enough that I have to stand on tiptoes to kiss him. Tall enough that he's perfectly at ease wandering around in flip-flops and board shorts, in keeping with our new boho-chic life by the beach. Sometimes I look at other men on the esplanade in their socks and sandals and tired polo shirts and picture Nevin wearing the same things. I marvel at how he would be able to pull it off without looking as sad and empty as these men.

I guess you could say he has a mysterious quality. Like he knows something that everyone else doesn't, yet probably should. That's what gets people intrigued, I think. How does this guy seem so at ease with everything that's going on in the world when most days I struggle to even get out of bed in the morning?

It's not that I'm depressed. Why would I be? But I have had to learn to cope with some pretty awful anxiety attacks that started the day I became a teenager. I've had to fight tooth and nail to project the image I do, and it has not been an easy ride.

Unlike Nevin I'm not blessed with this magical ability to coast through life, changing career whenever I want to and making a success of it. That's another infuriating thing about him. He'll suddenly become obsessed with something and then take it to the extreme until he's done with it, before casting it aside and moving on to the next dream.

Ten years ago, he woke up one morning and decided he wanted to be a music journalist, so did a desk swipe at his very decently paid job as a middle manager for a property company and by 5pm that evening had written his first article for *Q* Magazine. He didn't even ask for my opinion or support on the matter. He just did it.

With me, it's always taken months of planning to even consider a change like that. Hours every night spent researching and costing and projecting, writing pros and cons, talking to friends of friends who are in similar industries and building lists of contacts and tips for launching a business. And it wasn't until recently that I figured out why. It's all been with one thing in mind.

Projection.

The need to present to the world that I am a confident and successful woman, that I am exceptional, that I deserve everything that I have got and what is still to come. That's been my primary driving ambition since the day I saw *Working Girl* for the first time when I was eleven.

And now I have it all. A successful career, two beautiful children, a tall and quite handsome husband and a picture-book cottage by the sea.

So why do I still feel like something is missing? Something that stays with me deep into the night, when Nevin has long since rolled over and gone to sleep. Something that eats away at my confidence and erodes my self-belief to the extent that I have to get up the next morning and start all over again at Page One.

I've discussed this *ad nauseum* with my mother. She understands because she went through exactly the same search for validation. My dad was basically a carbon copy of Nevin, but without the success. He had that aura that made women flock to him, but unlike Nevin, my dad wasn't fussy about who he indulged with and took advantage of. It took a lot of willpower for my mother to leave him, but in the end she got up the courage to do just that. My dad did not take it well. He fell apart and died six years after the divorce, alone and destitute, having wronged pretty much everyone who was ever foolish enough to care about him.

And maybe that's what it is that's been bugging me. For all

his qualities Nevin is still a child at heart. He's a fantastic father and provider, don't get me wrong. I'm proud to stand next to him at social events and in photographs at family weddings, with our two angelic (ha!) children trying not to pull each other's arms off. And I've tried for so long to understand the mystery behind Nevin's countenance, the source of that unyielding confidence and assurance that no matter what happens he will cope with it.

It's because he thinks nobody would ever betray him. He honestly thinks that he's got it so made that nobody would ever have the guts or ability to take away everything that he has.

But he's wrong.

And there it is. The Achilles heel of our life together and the source of my current onslaught of anxiety.

It's because I know that taking everything away from him is exactly what I am about to do.

6

GLORIA

Nevin and I had actually known each other before we started dating as we both lived in the same small Hampshire town growing up. There was always some mild flirtation at social occasions, and by that I mean the pub on a Friday night, but usually we were with other partners so nothing ever came of it. Then we both moved away, as one does in one's early twenties, to focus on going out into the big wide world and carving our own career paths, and we didn't see each other at all for the next five years.

It wasn't until we randomly ran into each other in a bar one night in Bristol that we realised we were both single and both living nearby. Nevin was working for an architectural firm as some sort of research analyst, a job which he found remarkably boring. He was thinking of jacking it in and moving to France. That was the first thing he told me after striking up a conversation while we both ordered drinks.

I immediately found him intriguing. He seemed to have lost all the awkwardness of his youth, when he was quite gangly and suffered from acne. He had blossomed into this tall and pretty well-built Casanova type that I saw before me. He was wearing blue jeans and a blue Ralph Lauren shirt, which has since become his signature look when he isn't lounging around the house in shorts and T-shirt, and talked passionately about wanting to buy a smallholding in Lombardy and write crime novels.

He was five years older than me and approaching thirty, and in my inexperience I took him to be eminently knowledgeable on the subject of emigrating and setting up a successful career abroad.

At the time I was working for a publishing house editing self-help books, which didn't exactly offer world-beating career progression.

I had dropped out of my university course reading English just one year shy of graduating, mainly because I ran out of money and my mum could no longer afford to keep paying my rent in the exclusive spa town of Leamington in the Midlands. Which meant I was forced to look for any work I could get in a market vastly overcrowded by graduates in fairly useless subjects all vying for the same roles.

This was in the early noughties, when although university education in Britain was still paid for by the state, it still meant you had to self-fund three years of study through loans or your own savings. I had no savings and had racked up a fairly hefty student loan bill of fifteen thousand pounds, so the quicker I got a job and started paying that off the better. It was yet another period of my life when the thought of being self-sufficient and comfortably off was way out of my reach. But I had the exuberance of youth and the time that came with it, so I was just enjoying my life as much as I could. All my best friends were doing the same thing, and marriage and children were quite literally the last things on our minds at that stage in our lives.

But here came this attractive and intellectual guy with his

romantic dreams of life on a smallholding in a foreign land, and I have to say, I was hooked.

We dated casually for a few months, and by that I mean we hooked up on a Friday and Saturday night and got pissed in the pub with our mates before enjoying lazy Sundays in bed watching movies and talking about books. Nevin seemed impressed with my thirst for literature. He even suggested early on that I should become a literary agent. I obviously parked that in the back of my subconscious for later consideration.

But after the initial holiday period of the relationship, I became worried that I might not be enough for this enigmatic man, who thought nothing of throwing into the conversation how he was ready to get married and have kids. That five year age difference didn't seem like much at first, but while I was still in party mode in my mid-twenties it was clear that Nevin had already fleshed out the broader picture of his next ten or fifteen years.

I don't know if it was the urge to cling onto a seemingly good thing, or the need to prove to myself that I too was growing up and should take some responsibility for my own life, but I gave Nevin an ultimatum. I told him that if he was serious about me, he should do something about it, or I was going to go travelling around the Far East and didn't know if I would come back.

Part... okay, almost all of me, thought that he would wish me well with a pat on the bum and sod off to find his next plaything, but to my surprise he said he was deadly serious about me and said that we should move in together. He had bought a small, terraced house just outside the city, with two bedrooms and a quite disgustingly ill cat, and as his housemate was moving to London, he said he had the space. That's how Nevin and I ended up together, and how six months later I found myself pregnant.

I wasn't even worried that we weren't married, this was the

twenty-first century after all and who got married anymore? Until one day, after he had passed his exams to be a building surveyor (his latest infuriatingly easy career change), Nevin texted me out of the blue while I was at work and asked me to marry him.

Yes, *texted*.

I know that's not the most romantic of ways to pop the question, but it seemed perfectly in keeping with his carefree attitude to life. The fact that he didn't feel the need to make it ultra special, with a romantic dinner and flower petals on the bed, almost made it more special. More *unique* to us.

We talked about whether we should tie the knot before or after the baby came along. I was already starting to show, and the idea of squeezing into a wedding dress just a month before I was to give birth didn't fill me with anticipation, and also wouldn't it look like a shotgun wedding? As ever, Nevin said he didn't give two short shits about what anybody else thought. He wanted to do it in July when I would be eight months pregnant.

That's how I came to organise my entire wedding at short notice and with a rather large bun in my oven.

I think back to that time as I hang up the drinks menu, so lovingly illustrated by our daughter Amy on the rear deck of our home by the sea, wondering how I ever had such a dynamic and resourceful outlook to do such a thing. Especially when my hormones were raging and I was facing the prospect of a dry wedding, watching everyone else drink and have a great time while I stuck to soda and cranberry. Ah, the glorious purpose of youth. Would I ever do something like that today, as older and wiser as I am?

Well, if you call having an affair with my husband's oldest friend purposeful, then I suppose I would.

7

GLORIA

I know what you're thinking. You always have a choice. There's always a moment when you could just say 'No' and stop whatever is about to happen from, well, happening. If you think like that then you've got more strength than any real human I know. Truth is, we all like to think that we have that ability, that unshakeable sense of morality, but in practice the reality is a lot different. In the real heat of the moment, when all the cards are on the table, you always go with what your heart wants instead of what your head is telling you you should or should not do.

And it wasn't all my fault. There *were* other parties involved. And you know what, screw that, I'm not going to refer to it as a 'fault' anymore either. Sometimes you get pushed into something whether you like it or not, and the only thing you can do is let it play out and hope you don't hurt too many people along the way. But life is your own, you can only live it your way, and sometimes in the pursuit of your own happiness you have to accept that you might make other people unhappy with your actions.

There, that's my little speech of justification. Now onto the details.

I first met Felix, my husband's best friend, when Nevin introduced us not long after I became pregnant. As it had become clear to him that Nevin was serious about our relationship (and with a baby on the way and a wedding to plan it didn't get much more serious), Felix had insisted on taking us both out to dinner to celebrate and to actually meet the woman who was responsible for snaring his oldest mate in her web and getting him to settle down.

My first thought was: *what an arrogant prick.*

Felix arrived at the restaurant in a full three-piece tweed suit, which was quite beautifully tailored, and so cleanly shaved and so coiffured that I assumed he had just come straight from the barber. He was very, very good-looking, with a face like a young Roger Moore and the distinguished air of Rex Harrison. But he was way too loud and brash for my pregnancy-sensitive ears, and I honestly thought he was putting on some kind of initial act before he would actually settle down and become his normal self.

'Daaarling!' he cooed at me, 'I stand in a moment of exquisite delight as I finally get to meet Helen of Troy!' before taking my hand in his and delicately kissing it. Then he looked up at me and in total seriousness said, 'Fuck that! Come here, you gorgeous creature!' before taking me in his arms, sweeping me backwards and planting a huge kiss right on my mouth. His skin was smooth and cool, his lips surprisingly dry and supple, and he smelled of a very expensive cologne. Although I could detect the aroma of whisky on his breath.

He then did something even stranger. Leaning around me he raised both his hands and placed them tenderly on the sides of Nevin's face. Looking deeply into Nevin's eyes he slowly kissed both cheeks of his face like a long-lost lover. I knew they were close, but this gesture seemed a little too intimate for even my liberal mind to grapple with.

I was a little in shock to say the least, but Nevin just looked on as if this kind of elaborate show of affection was perfectly normal. He had warned me in the taxi that Felix could be a touch *theatrical* at times, but I wasn't expecting a character straight out of *Don Juan*. I just put it down to spending too many years in the company of flirtatious European types.

But his display of blatant flirtation extended beyond me to the waitresses and even the Maître d', who could only shyly giggle when Felix introduced him as 'the most outstanding sommelier since Lepeltier.'

When we finally sat down at the table Felix did ease off the dramatics slightly, and I actually found him to be very interesting company. He certainly knew how to compliment a woman, and I found myself drawn to him more and more as the meal went on and he gave me his undivided attention. I actually got a little concerned at one point that he seemed to be almost completely neglecting Nevin and focusing entirely on me. Not only did his compliments fly, on my hair, my dress, my glowing skin, but he seemed genuinely fascinated by everything I talked about from my love of literature to where I grew up. Somehow he even coaxed out of me whether or not I was wearing a bra (I wasn't) and how I lost my virginity, even making me feel totally at ease when describing the experience. Something I hadn't even told Nevin by that point.

By the end of the night I felt a little empty when we said our goodbyes and it was just me and Nevin again in the back of the taxi. Nevin grinned broadly when he saw the look on my face.

'I told you, didn't I?' he said smugly. 'That's Felix through and through. He makes you feel like you're the only person in the world that matters. Then...' He blew through his fingers like Keyser Söze at the end of *The Usual Suspects*, 'he's gone...'

'He's certainly a character,' I admitted.

'He's a fucking *liability*,' said Nevin with a laugh. 'He's okay in small doses. I guess you kind of understand why we don't see each other that much now.'

'Is he always so... elaborate?' I asked.

'That was nothing. You should be grateful you're not single, then you would have seen him pull out all the stops.'

Nevin must have seen the mild surprise in my eyes, because he laughed and kissed me on the side of my head. 'The important thing to know is that he's harmless. He's a philandering, single-minded, boorish wanker when it comes to women, but if he's on your side he's there for life.'

Nevin leaned back in the rear of the taxi and immediately began to doze off the port and whisky he'd put back with dinner.

Later, as I fell asleep myself, lying next to Nevin in the little terraced house we now shared with his ailing cat, I couldn't help but wonder over and over what Felix would be like in bed.

8
―――
NEVIN

So the party is in full swing, and I'm having a crafty cigarette in the garage just to escape the noise for a few moments. In the garden I can hear the strains of 'Bohemian Rhapsody' kick off and everyone starts singing Freddie Mercury at the top of their lungs. I can't stop a grin forming on my face as I imagine the scenes. I think that's the only genuine grin that I've managed today. The rest have been hard work as I struggle to live up to expectations of greeting the mass of friends and family that has descended on our perfect garden and into the marquee to escape the blazing sun that has graced us with its presence on this, my big day.

My only way of coping with such a boisterous social occasion is the five minutes of each hour that I've allowed myself to sneak off to enjoy a nicotine injection in the privacy of my garage. The flower-beds have also been copiously overwatered with the hose by the front door.

I've never been particularly good at parties. Sure I'm able to project the image of being totally at ease in my surroundings, making idle small talk with Gloria's man-hating aunt or discussing stock options with the obligatory group of dads that have turned up with their kids in tow as playmates for Amy and Josh. But it all just seems so contrived. Everyone is there decked out to the nines in their summer outfits, and it won't be until at least six o'clock tonight when everyone is sufficiently full of booze that their realness will appear and they'll actually start having a good time without worrying about their appearance in the eyes of the other guests.

At least the kids seem to be enjoying themselves. There's a Spanish guitar duo scheduled to play later on which should be... entertaining. Two guys in their twenties in wide-brimmed hats who, at the request of Gloria, will play a selection of flamenco songs. How Gloria managed to find them is a mystery to me, but apparently they've travelled down from Kent. Which isn't really surprising given the amount we are paying them.

'It'll be worth it for the atmosphere!' Gloria had told me when she confirmed the booking. Personally I can't see how replacing a banging selection of eighties rock hits chugging through a massive PA system with two acoustic guitars and cries of *Baila Me!* is going to bring the house down, but as usual I just went with the flow and said it was a great idea. I learned long ago that pooh-poohing one of my wife's ideas straight off the bat is a dangerous game, no matter how absurd the idea might be.

And the truth is, I am grateful for the effort she's put in to making this whole occasion work. It's just that I never asked for it in the first place. I'm doing it more for the kids, to make the day something they will never forget. Birthday parties post-forty? I can take 'em or leave 'em. And I just know I'm going to have to pull something special out of the bag for Gloria's fortieth.

If we ever make it that far.

I'm momentarily distracted by the sight of a man on a bicycle coming up the lane towards our driveway. Judging by the expensive bike and the lithe body clad in skintight yellow Lycra, it can only be one person.

My best mate Felix has joined the party.

Instead of rushing out to greet him I skulk slightly further back in the garage, behind an old chest of drawers that we haven't found a place for yet in the cottage, and secrete myself out of view.

It's just like Felix to make a fashionably late entrance to a party, looking like he's just come fresh off a leg of the Tour de France. Christ, the mums are going to go wild when they see him in all that Lycra.

Felix is my oldest buddy, and thus, given that I am still in contact with him, I suppose you could term him my best friend. Unlike Gloria, who is able to flit through acquaintances with the ease of a honeybee landing on the sweetest flowers, I only have two or maybe three people who I consider real friends. To be honest, I just don't have the energy for any more than that. Men are wired differently when it comes to long-term friendships. I can easily go a year without speaking to Felix, but when we do on occasion pick up the phone to each other or actually go the whole hog and meet up for drinks, it's like we are still sharing a room back at university. The old jokes, reminiscing over old conquests, stuff like that. That's the beauty of a 'childhood' friend, you don't have to keep up appearances and discuss finances and cars and schools and all the mundane things that you feel obliged to cover when you're talking to other guys in their forties who you've just met.

Yeah I know it sounds immature, but show me a married guy who doesn't hanker after his youth before marriage and kids, and all the simplicity it afforded before the stresses of life got in the way, and I'll show you a very deluded man. My friendship with Felix is built on years of that kind of nostalgia.

There's no way you'd catch us talking about something as mature as an ISA or buying a new Tesla on finance.

But today I want to let him have his entrance and his fifteen minutes of being gawped at by the female attendees, from the teenage daughters to the grandmas in their sixties and seventies, not to mention probably my own wife. Then I'll grab him for my own purposes. I know he'll be way too distracted looking drop-dead gorgeous in his cycling gear and making the women swoon to pay me much attention, at least until he's got a couple of beers in him.

I see him gingerly rest his precious bike, all three grand's worth of it, against a patch of wall that has an overhanging section of moss so he doesn't risk scratching the carbon finish. Honestly, who shows up to a Spanish-themed birthday party dressed as Lance Armstrong?

Felix is one of those rare creatures who has coasted through life managing to avoid any real responsibility. His father was a successful politician, who even served in the cabinet at one point and was appointed a Lord in the outgoing Prime Minister's honours list in the 1970s. Since he died, Felix is entitled to use The Right Honourable before his name, though, to his credit, he never does. But although you would assume he comes from money, and his lifestyle certainly supports that image, he's actually as broke as a church mouse. He lives off the generosity of his connections, one of whom I'm sorry to say is me. I lost count of the amount of 'cheeky tenners' I lent him at uni, and would rather not think about the cheeky *hundreds* that I've spotted him almost every year since then.

The thing about Felix is, none of that matters. The bastard is infectious, and one whose company is so enjoyable that you find yourself willing to sign over your life savings after spending ten minutes talking to him, just to make him stay a bit longer. He has the irresistible ability to sound like the most fascinating person in the world, while at the same time making you feel like you're the only person in the world. When he gives you his full attention, it takes almost superhuman strength to pull yourself away.

I watch silently as he adjusts his wavy blond hair in the bike's tiny mirror. It is always set perfectly, even when he takes off his absurdly streamlined cycling helmet. I bet he smells of Paco Rabanne aftershave. He flicks a wink and a finger point at himself in the mirror, with the permanent slight grin of a man who is always scouting for his next meal ticket.

You have to give him credit: if he sees something he wants, he more often than not gets it. He is the most addictive son of a bitch you'll ever meet, and therefore the most frustrating. But it was good of him to cut into his schedule of semi-professional competitive cycling around Europe to make it to my fortieth.

This party might not be so dull after all.

9

GLORIA

I'm stuck in a less than riveting conversation with a group of female friends in the garden when I see Felix sauntering up the pathway looking like a million dollars. He instantly sees me and weaves his way in our direction, grinning from ear to ear. I knew he was coming, but despite all the planning that we went through before the event I still can't believe that he's had the stones to show up. And the dread about giving him the news that I'm pregnant with his child almost makes me light-headed.

God, I wish I could have a drink. I've had to give the old excuse of being on antibiotics for an unspecified infection as the reason why I'm only drinking sparkling water at my husband's fortieth birthday party.

'Who is *that*?' says Lydia, gawping, a frumpy woman who rather annoyingly runs the book club I like to attend every Thursday evening in town. She is already three sheets to the wind, and it's only 2pm.

'Oh,' I say as off-handedly as I can manage. 'That's Felix. Nevin's oldest friend from university.'

'Felix Van Arnhem?' says Anna, the town librarian, a

woman in her sixties who I felt obliged to invite since I spend so much time at her establishment borrowing and returning books, and who clearly subscribes to social lifestyle magazines. 'He is *gorgeous*. I think my ovaries just skipped a beat.'

I cringe at her imagery, thinking a) of a sixty-year-old woman's ovaries and b) how ironic her comment is given my current situation. But she's right. Felix looks utterly amazing in his full cycling gear. I had hoped he would play down his propensity for grand entrances, but who was I kidding? This was Felix.

The Lycra shorts don't just show off every toned muscle in his tanned thighs, they almost make a presentation of them. I just know every woman in this garden right now is checking out the bulge at the front of them, and probably a few of the more envious men present as well. And that's before you get to the washboard abs that are virtually screaming to be let loose from his jersey (I swear you can see the outline of his six-pack through the bright yellow material) and continue up to his broad pectorals and equally impressive shoulders. My mouth instantly goes dry with excitement, which is the opposite of what usually happens. The sight of him naked usually makes me salivate.

I thought Nevin had charisma, but Felix? He's at least three levels higher. What the two of them must have got up to as bachelors at university I don't want to imagine right now. All I can think of is how I need that man on top of me, and how I'm going to make that happen later on tonight.

As subtly as I can I try to draw myself away from the gaggle of horny women I'm standing with and make my way towards him. But my feet seem to be rooted to the spot, as if unable to move given the glorious sight of this man Mick Jaggering his way up the path.

Some men improve with age. Felix definitely proves that

theory. If he looks this good at forty, just imagine when his hair goes a bit greyer round the temples and that sexy salt-and-pepper stubble in his beard goes full-on salt. I could honestly say that if George Clooney himself walked into the garden party right now he'd get no more than a side glance from most of the assembled guests.

Jesus, I have to pull myself together or I'm going to have to go and change my panties.

'Ladiiiies!' he says, oozing charm as he approaches us. 'And I thought the view was spectacular *before* I walked into the garden.'

'Um, girls, this is Felix, Nevin's oldest friend,' I manage to stutter out while the other women make a great show of oohing and aahing in surprise, as if they didn't already know this fact. Honestly, it's like a scene from *Desperate Housewives*.

'An honour it surely is to make your acquaintance,' says Felix smoothly as he nods his head at each and every one of the group in turn, meeting their gaze with his stunning deep-green eyes. I can't stop myself from humming *Jeepers creepers, where'd you get those peepers* under my breath. He finishes up on me, before smiling demurely and leaning in to give me a kiss on both cheeks. As he pulls away he mutters, 'You look good enough to consume whole,' just quietly enough that the rest of the group don't hear. I think.

'Now who do I have to fuck to get a drink in this place?' he says laughing, and then looks slightly guiltily at my daughter Amy who is rushing over to greet him.

'Uncle Fixly!' she shouts in pure joy. Even kids fall under this man's spell. Do I really need to explain the origins of that nickname? Okay, when the kids were small they had trouble saying Felix, and he had been Uncle Fixly ever since.

'Monstress!' he shouts back, gathering her up in his two per cent fat arms and swinging her around. 'Crikey, you've got big! When did you turn into Barbie?'

Amy squeals in delight, and I marvel at Felix's knowledge of my little girl's current favourite movie character. She has done her golden-blonde hair up in a single long flowing ponytail in a very deliberate attempt to look like Margot Robbie.

'We've got a piñata! Come and see, come and see!' Amy says excitedly.

'All in good time, my little dove. How's about you go and grab your Uncle Fixer-Wixer a beer first, eh?'

'Okay!' she says jumping up and down, before running off to the bar thrilled that she's been asked to do something grown-up for a change. As if being in charge of the bar menu wasn't enough for a twelve-year-old, something I was less than happy about Nevin allowing.

There is a slightly awkward moment of silence as Felix turns back to the group and none of the women present can think of anything to say while they stare at him.

As ever it is Felix who brings the mood back. 'Now then! Where is the old bastard?' he says, craning his head around in search of Nevin.

'Oh, er, I think he must have gone in the house to get more ice or something. Did you not see him on your way in?' I ask.

'Parked the carbon steed by the garage and came up the old side path, didn't I?' he says in his mellifluous voice. Everything that Felix says is touched with a degree of ridiculousness that only he can pull off.

'You came on a *motorbike?*' says Anna as if it were the most daredevil thing she'd ever heard of.

'Christ no,' he replies, 'motorbikes are for Ulstermen. I pedal-powered my way here direct from the Bahnhof. Which does mean I didn't have space for an overnight bag. Guess I'll just have to sleep in the old N.U.D.E,' he says, spelling out the word and winking directly at me. I widen my eyes in anger at him for being so openly flirtatious.

Amy returns with his beer and drags him off to see the piñata, which is hanging at the entrance of the marquee. A group of about fifteen kids are gazing up at it longingly, waiting to be given the all-clear to finally bash it open and get at the sweets inside. I should clarify with Nevin that it would definitely be a good plan to let them do this earlier on in the day. Last thing we want is a major sugar-high in a bunch of pre-teens before bedtime.

Speaking of Nevin, where the heck is he? I know he hates social occasions at the best of times, but when the whole thing is centred around him it makes him cringe even more. I suppose you could say that's another one of his 'qualities'. He's very good at downplaying his ego. But this is his birthday party, and everyone here is here for him, so the least he could do is actually mingle and let them know he is grateful. Some of the guests have travelled quite a way to be here after all.

I bet he's smoking in the garage again. He thinks I don't know he does this, and even tries to disguise it by keeping a bottle of mouthwash hidden behind a cabinet in there, but I'm not stupid. He 'gave up' three years ago when the kids cottoned onto the fact that it's a disgusting habit and very damaging to a person's health, and they hated seeing him do it. But he found it very hard, and even put on quite a bit of weight at first as he overcompensated for the craving with food. He lost it again just as quickly by simply going on a brown rice diet for two weeks. The man's willpower when he wants to achieve something is quite astonishing.

I see him emerge from the garden path and make his way slowly back into the crowd, and try to catch his eye to let him know that Felix actually made it after all. But I guess he'll figure that out for himself soon enough.

And then the fun will really start.

Nevin and Felix together is usually a combination for trouble.

Throw an unlimited supply of booze into the equation, and you have a recipe for disaster.

10

GLORIA

I guess at this point I should tell you how my affair with Felix started.

It's not uncommon for someone to get involved with their spouse's best friend, just so you know. It happens a lot. And while that doesn't justify our behaviour, I like to believe it goes some way to mitigating it.

It's not hard to see why these things happen. A best friend after all is like an extension of your partner, but without all the mess that comes with them. They are often similar in character. That's usually why they migrate to each other's company in the first place.

You see the same qualities in them as you do in your partner, but without the grind of having to live with them all the time and put up with their foibles on a daily basis. A best friend can make you hark back to that magical time when you first got together with your partner, when you were just getting to know all the little things that made you fall in love with them. These things are often mirrored in the friend, and you get to almost relive with that friend that time before you became accustomed to and accepting of your partner's faults. It can be very enlightening.

But it can also be very dangerous. It can make you think that you plumped for second best, when in fact you should have gone with the best friend in the first place...

Women who are best friends share everything. Emotionally, physically, all their hopes and dreams, all their bugbears and complaints, they let it all spill out without any filter. Women aren't afraid of being vulnerable in front of other women as they know they will get the empathy and support they crave from another human of a similar mind.

Men are different though. When two men make friends with each other they will often go out of their comfort zone in order to make the other like them even more. To fit in with their world view and to be accepted as an equal. I guess it goes back to the days when we all lived in caves, and only the strongest and most adept hunters would bag the women. I know that's a fairly animalistic way of looking at it, and of course humankind has developed far beyond that thanks to the introduction of politics, literature and religion, but at heart men are basically primal creatures. They want to eat, mate and sleep. Anything else on top of that is just bells and whistles.

Like the notion of keeping your woman happy for example.

That's the thing about Nevin. As long as he is happy, he just assumes that everyone else around him is too. I'm not saying he's been a bad husband. He has always provided for us, and he did take one for the team with this move away from our little-too-comfortable life in the city. I know he wasn't keen on upsetting the apple cart, and he did recognise something within me that needed to do it. Perhaps not just for the benefit of the kids, but for my own sanity. And he gets the concept of monogamy. Yes, I know that's rich coming from me. But as far as I know he has never strayed. I just don't think he would have the energy or gumption to cope with more than one woman.

But sometimes being a good man just isn't enough. I know there are millions of women who would disagree with me, and who would kill to be married to a guy like Nevin. But it's all relative isn't it? One woman's hell is another's heaven and all that?

I'm not passing the buck here. I know it takes two to tango, and I am, perhaps, just as responsible for events taking the turn they did. Believe me, I've gone over this in my head a thousand times trying to find the justification for my actions. My mind is like yin and yang, it works both best and worst at night. When everyone else in the house is fast asleep, I'm the one who lies awake going over and over in my head how to solve this problem and that problem, and never really coming to a satisfying outcome. As Nevin will often say to me when we argue, 'Everything is fine until you *think* of a problem.'

I suppose what I'm getting at here is that I've never really thought Nevin *believed* in me. And that lack of faith from someone to whom you have entrusted your life is very hard to accept. He thinks I'm like my mother, flighty and fickle, brushing off the real issues in favour of appearances.

To a certain extent he's right, but at least I acknowledge my own flaws and I try to better them all the time, whereas Nevin just expects everybody else to fit in to his mould. If they don't like it, they can lump it. And while that is an enviable world outlook to have (I wish to God I had it), it doesn't make for a well-rounded, adjusted human being in my view. Nevin would rather starve than eat what someone expected him to eat. Just for the sake of bucking the trend.

It wasn't until only recently that I figured my husband out. Nevin thinks he's the exception to the rule. That nobody and nothing is going to tell him what to do or how to do it.

Apart from Felix.

My husband is a totally different person around Felix. In other company he will happily sit in his shell and be silent for hours rather than do the socially accepted thing and make conversation. Just because he can. Until Felix is around it's like he can't break those shackles and really emerge from his chrysalis.

For example, I want to take the kids paddleboarding. We live by the beach now for Christ's sake, it's something that we should take advantage of. Nevin will instantly pooh-pooh the idea and talk about how much paddleboards cost. I say no matter, I'll buy it, I'm starting to make good money now. He'll say fine, but then retreat into his shell again because it wasn't his idea and he's not the one to make it financially possible. He'd rather sit in his dingy little garage behind his desk (solid mahogany no less) and write a few thousand words of his latest novel (this one's going to be a bestseller, Glor, I can feel it!) than actually live a little and take his kids down the beach so we can enjoy ourselves as a family.

But I just bet, in fact I *know,* that if Felix turned up here one day with a paddleboard in tow, then Nevin would be the first into his wetsuit. Even if the kids weren't going. In fact, he'd probably make some excuse as to why me and the kids *couldn't* come, just so he could have his precious time with Felix.

God, I sound like a nightmare don't I? First world problems and all that? My pearl necklace is too small! My dog got mud all over the new Defender!

I'm not like that, I promise. I just want what's best for my family, and to enjoy my kids while they are still at the age where they actually want to spend time with their parents. Nevin seems to be looking forward to the kids leaving home so they aren't such a burden on him every day, and I've just never understood that. I'm not saying he doesn't love his kids. He's great with them. When he actually gets round to spending time with them and he and Felix aren't off on another cycling weekend around Ireland...

So I hatched a plan. At first I wasn't sure I would even go through with it, but it helped to have something working in my mind. It was my intention to make Nevin see what he really had, and why it was so precious.

Sleeping with Felix was easy. I mean, come on. I'm in my prime and the man is a walking erection. He's nearly forty, never been married, has no kids (that we are aware of) and even if he did he certainly isn't interested in them. I simply arranged to be on a work trip in Hamburg the very week I knew he would be there taking part in the Deutschland Tour.

First I waited until Nevin was on the phone to Felix one evening. He claims they don't speak that often, but I know he's down in his garage on the phone at least once a week because I can hear him laughing through the walls. He never laughs on the phone unless it's with Felix.

I went out to the garage with a bag of laundry to stick in the washing machine, and the second I walked in Nevin instantly became much more serious and began discussing cycling. *Twat,* I thought. He doesn't even *like* cycling. He abhors physical exercise in all forms, which is yet another infuriating thing about him as he always manages to stay a steady thirteen stone. While the rest of us have to actually work out to maintain our bodies, he'd rather just not eat for a week if he feels he's put on a couple of pounds.

After he hung up, I said casually, 'What's Felix been up to?'

Nevin instantly became defensive, as if he'd been rumbled. He thought I didn't know who he was talking to.

'Good, yeah, he's good. He's off on another of his cycling tours next week.' He rolled his eyes as if this was a crushing bore to him.

'Oh yeah? Where's he headed this time?'

Nevin pretended to have gone back to work on his computer. 'Hmm? Oh, Germany. Hamburg I think.'

'That's interesting. I'm in Hamburg next week as well.'

'Are you?' said Nevin, with a little concern creeping into his voice.

'Yeah, I'm going to work through the contract with Hildebrand. Looks like I've finally got her on board. I told you the other day, remember?' I hadn't told him any such thing, but I was banking on his usual desire to avoid a tense conversation.

'Of course, yes, of course. Well, you two should get together and have some dinner or something. Don't worry about me and the kids, we'll be fine.'

He had to throw that in there, didn't he? A little dig insinuating that I was abandoning the family yet again to focus on my work. I could have said something like he should be happy for me as things were really falling into place business-wise for me, but I wasn't going to give him the satisfaction of rising to it.

'What, me and Felix?' I said instead. 'You wouldn't mind?'

'Why on earth would I mind?' said Nevin, looking up in mild surprise from his screen.

'It's just that you don't get to see him that often, and I thought you might feel left out if it was me having all the fun with him and not you.'

I knew he wouldn't rise to this. Any emotion other than solid indifference was what I was expecting, and what I got.

'Don't be silly! You should definitely hit the town while you're there. It's not all work, work, work you know.'

Oh the irony, coming from a man who would rather write about Cold War dead letter drops than take his kids to the beach.

'Okay then,' I said. 'I'll give Felix a call and arrange

something.' Just to be extra sweet, I gave Nevin a little peck on the cheek and said, 'Thank you, honey, you're such a good husband.'

As I left I could almost feel him bristling behind me.

11

FELIX

I could get used to small-town life. I felt certain this party would be boring as holy heck, with vicars and cucumber sandwiches and farmers discussing cider. But I have to hand it to my old buddy Nevin. He never skimps when it comes to a knees-up. Some of the women here aren't half bad. A touch dowdy and provincial for my tastes, but when you're used to millionaire divorcees swinging off the side of yachts in Monte Carlo then most things appear that way at first. And even the vicar's wife can get a bit frisky after a few glasses of bubbly. If she's encouraged the right way...

You might think, *what a bastard*. And you'd be right to a certain extent. But I'll let you in to a little secret; it isn't actually easy being me. I'm really no different to your average forty-something bloke who projects an image of financial security and marital bliss in the suburbs, yet who is slowly dying inside. You know the guy, who gets up every morning and commutes to his job in the city and flirts with his secretary and maybe even gives her one on the side every now and again but at the end of the day returns home as the trusty breadwinner and loving father and husband?

There are a million blokes like that in this country alone. And they're all projecting an image. The image of respectability and propriety. Of *fitting in*.

I just project a different kind of image.

One of wealth, jet-settery and a playboy lifestyle with a line of mistresses the length of Southend Pier.

You think it's easy doing what I do? You should try it. I get pathetic little men telling me how great it must be being me, living it up in a different European city every week, eating out in expensive restaurants and dangling my toes in the Aegean off luxury boats. 'Why can't I do that?' they ask.

And my internal response to each and every one is *Fuck off, you spineless little excuse for a man*. Instead I say, 'If you really want to do it that badly, then do it.'

'Oh I couldn't,' they say, 'I've got responsibilities, a family, bills to pay!'

You don't think I have responsibilities? You think I take this shit lightly? You think it's *easy* schmoozing through life without knowing where you're going to be this time next week?

I'll tell you right now, it isn't. But I've been doing it for so long that I don't know how to do anything else.

Let me tell you a little bit about The Right Honourable Felix Aloysius Van Arnhem.

At boarding school my nickname was Bean. Get it? My initials are FAVA. But it was also because I was tall and wiry, and would go green at the thought of eating the vegetables – we weren't allowed to leave the table until we had finished.

My father was in the House of Lords, which in the UK doesn't mean that much anymore. The way things are going soon there won't be any Lords left, but in the 1980s it was a pretty big deal. And because of who my old man was, I was expected to achieve. It didn't matter so much that I was too lanky to be in the first XV rugby team, too socially awkward to chair the debating society, or even that I preferred the mystery of the stage and performing in the school theatre. As long as I achieved academically and did what was expected of me then I would have *fitted in*. And that was going to Oxford or Cambridge to read politics and following in my old man's footsteps.

My life was planned out for me before I was even born. And when you have an old man like mine, you had better toe the line or you would get a damn good cuff around the lugholes. That means a beating, for those of you who don't speak public school.

My dad never really involved himself in my life at all until the end-of-term report cards came in, when he would sit in his study at his Mousey Thompson desk and, with his reading glasses perched superciliously on the end of his nose, scrutinise every single comment written about young Felix by my teachers.

He needs to apply himself more.

He believes the rules by which we operate do not apply to him.

And my favourite, from my old housemaster Bugger Lloyd: *Felix is devious, amoral and unscrupulous. He will make an excellent MP.*

Then I would be summoned, given a stern lecture on the importance of academic attainment and the consequences of failure, and be vigorously lashed on my bare bottom so hard I had to take salt baths for a week afterwards to alleviate the pain. And this was an unending cycle, three times a year until I hit sixteen and was considered too big for an arse-whooping. When that happened, it wasn't physical punishment that my father doled out, but verbal disappointment. And let me tell you, a tongue-lashing from my pops hurt just as much as one from the cane.

I didn't get into Oxford or Cambridge, needless to say. And

that was the last straw for my father. He pointed to the door and said 'Son – and that is the last time I will call you that – I don't care how you make your way through life, just as long as I never hear about it.'

What more motivation does a young man need?

I think the fact that my younger brother Edward was doing exactly what was expected of him made my dramatic exile from the family even more gratifying for my father. Otherwise, with the continued success of the family name at stake, he might actually have given me some support and guidance. Not that I would have taken it. My father cut me off in every sense, paternally, practically and financially.

But not socially.

I still had his name. And the name Van Arnhem opened a lot of doors in those days. Any door it opens now is solely down to me, since my father went bankrupt in 1998 and spent the last five years of his life drinking cheap red wine and falling asleep at cricket matches.

I knew that if my father was cutting me off I would need to find my own way of hustling in life. So, I used my years at university in Durham (itself a very respectable institution) to network, bluff and fornicate my way up the social food chain. If a girl's father wasn't in the government, the aristocracy or a millionaire many times over, she wouldn't get a look-in. Of course, they had to be good-looking to start with. If you're ugly then you're ugly. Men don't walk around with X-rays to see your 'inner beauty'.

Durham Uni was a hotbed of posh young fillies who were too dim to get into Oxbridge (much like myself) but who had unlimited access either to their own trust funds or their parents' credit cards (unlike myself). Their fathers couldn't get enough of me given my surname, but if it ever came to the point where one of these girls was getting a little too serious and insisting on being taken home to meet *my* dear old papa, well, it was 'Thank you and goodbye Camilla Mornington-Duckworth.'

It helped that by this stage I had grown into my height and now filled out a suit rather splendidly. I kept in physical shape by rowing and the odd gym session to bulk up, and by the time I graduated I had a little black book as thick as the works of Shakespeare.

The major advantage of a private school education in Britain is one's automatic inclusion in a stuffy and elite, but completely intangible organisation known as the Old Boys' Network. The great thing about it is that it doesn't exist on paper, but if you are in it you can ask any other member to do you a favour and it's considered spectacularly bad form to refuse.

My twenties were spent on a varying diet of free lunches, shooting weekends and skiing holidays all generously provided by simply showing up in the correct attire and telling people who I was. I was a sort of social dilettante who arrived late, ate the smoked salmon, drank the Veuve Clicquot, shagged the hostess and left with nary a word, and because no occasion was deemed fashionable enough if someone like me wasn't there, and as there were only a few of us, the invites kept pouring in.

Nobody even asked me that God-awful question 'So what do you dooo?' because they knew I didn't really do anything, and they didn't care. I effectively had a social golden ticket to go anywhere as long as I allowed myself to be photographed with the hosts. You may even have seen me in some of the glossier lifestyle magazines that were the bibles of the elite classes in the 90s and 00s. *Tatler, Vanity Fair* and *SLOAN!* I believe I even made it into *Vogue* once or twice when I spent some time in New York living with the heiress to a lipstick empire.

This was all fun and games until I hit thirty-five and realised that even if my looks weren't fading (if anything they were improving the more rugged and mature I became) it couldn't go on forever. I had spent the best part of two decades living a very glamorous but rootless existence and had absolutely zilch to show for it. I was excellent at spending other people's money, but useless at making my own. My eligibility as a bachelor was fading with each moon cycle as more and more of my acquaintances finally found the perfect wealthy mare and settled down to do what the privileged absolutely must do in order to perpetuate – breed.

And it occurred to me one day, as I sat on the terrace at La Rascasse in Monte Carlo sipping a vodka martini and fending off the advances of a charming-but-pushing-sixty former actress, maybe it was time indeed for me to settle down and find a place of my own to call home.

And it was at that precise moment that I got a call from Gloria Campbell, the wife of my Durham Uni roommate and oldest buddy Nevin, telling me she was in Hamburg next week and that she'd love to meet up.

What very fortuitous timing, I thought, as a plan began to form in my head.

12

NEVIN

I'm being shaken awake by small hands. Slowly I open my eyes and wince as the early morning sunshine leaks its way into them and stabs at the inside of my head.

Shit, I must have gone to bed without drawing the curtains.

I'm in that median world between asleep and awake, when you haven't fully processed yet quite where you are and what state of mind you are in.

'Daddy,' whispers Amy from the floor beside me. 'I'm hungry.'

I lean up and moan inwardly as consciousness comes back and I remember who I am and why I feel like I do. I'm in my bed, which is always a good sign. But the pounding in my head suggests that I definitely overindulged on something the night before. As I sit up further it all floods back.

Well, not all of it.

I don't remember going to bed for a start, but I'm here so I mustn't have got so drunk that I collapsed somewhere in the garden.

'Okay honey, just give Daddy a minute to wake up.'

Amy nods quietly and runs out of the room. I check the

alarm clock beside the bed and see it's only 7am. Jesus, how are the kids already up? I'm pretty sure we let them stay up past midnight, and therefore thought (naively) that it would afford us a bit of a lie-in come the morning. It's always the way with kids. On a school day you virtually have to drag them out of their pits in order to get them ready for school by 8.30am, but as soon as half-term rolls around and we become even slightly laxer with their bedtimes, they're awake and raring to go before sun up every day.

At least they are that little bit older now, and their morning routines don't have to be so closely supervised. My mind flashes back to the days when one of us, inevitably Gloria, would have to get up at the crack of dawn every day to make sure they didn't kill each other before breakfast. Now they are a bit more independent and can actually fend for themselves in those first couple of early hours before the adults make an appearance.

But I remember expressly telling them before they settled that there was leftover food in the fridge and it would be fantastic if just for once they didn't wake us up this morning until we were ready.

Obviously Amy has no concept of a hangover at her age and so is quite happy shaking me awake when she feels I've had a long enough lie-in. That means the kids must have been awake for at least an hour already, which in turn means they probably only got a few hours' sleep, and further means they'll probably be as grumpy as hell today. But that's fine. If I know my hangovers, and I think this is going to be a fairly bad one, they can have a screen day while we go about recovering from one heck of a party.

I lean across to the other side of the bed expecting to feel Gloria's warm body slumbering next to me, but she isn't there. I take a few seconds to process this. As I said, I'd had way too much whisky last night and had no recollection of us going to bed, so can't remember if we went in together or I'd simply hit my limit and dragged myself off to sleep.

Oh well, if Gloria's up she is most likely dealing with the kids, so maybe I can go back to sleep for a couple of hours. I think about hauling myself out of bed to assess the damage to the lawn and see how many stragglers are left over from last night. We'd said people were welcome to stay if they wanted, they just had to bring a sleeping bag as we wouldn't have any room in the house, and I'm sure there will be a few slumbering bodies of the less responsible attendees in the marquee. Those who didn't live close enough by to make it to their own homes and were too cheap to book into one of the exclusive hotels that line the esplanade in town.

I half expect someone to stroll into my bedroom with an open bottle of champagne and demand that I partake in some hair of the dog. That's not a bad idea. I gag slightly at the thought of taking a sip of anything but a large glass of water and a couple of Alka-Seltzer, but to be perfectly honest if someone came in right now with a mimosa cocktail and a bacon sandwich I'd bite their arm off.

But the urge to rest takes over my body and I lay my head back down on the pillow to try and stop the pounding ache that's starting to realise it can really go to town on my dehydrated and overindulged head.

I can't tell if I drift off again or just enter into a period of wilful meditation, but whatever it is I'm jerked out of it again by Josh this time, as he comes in carrying his obligatory Rubik's cube and tries to show me his new record solving time.

'That's great, buddy. Why don't you go and show Mummy in the kitchen?' I groan.

That's when the memory of something dreadful hits me like a slug to the brain, and I jerk up in bed in horror. I squint my eyes and moan, 'No, no, no,' as the recollection of how the night ended comes back to me.

Gloria. And Felix.

Together.

In the summer house at the bottom of the garden.

The memory is desperately hazy at first, and my brain fizzes as it struggles to wrestle back the picture of my best friend and my wife going at it among the pile of yoga mats in the old wooden hut that we keep our garden supplies in.

'Oh shit,' I murmur. A wave of anxiety pours over me and my gorge rises once more as the events of last night rush back and devastate me all over again.

'Where's your mother?' I demand as I barge rather too quickly for my stomach to handle into the living room.

There's about ten kids, ranging from the ages of five to about fifteen, all sitting in a row with their faces buried in screens, like some kind of mass meditation ritual at a monastery. Only Josh doesn't have an iPad in front of him and is instead furiously fiddling with his cube in his eternal attempt to break the world solving record.

Amy looks up, a little in shock at the tone of my voice and not expecting to see an adult up and about. 'She's not here,' she says quietly, and goes back to her screen.

'What? Well where is she?' I say, trying to gather myself together. I must look quite a sight. I'm still wrapped in a Clint Eastwood-style poncho and my hair is pointing stupidly in every compass direction.

'Daddy, what happened to your face?' says Josh, looking up with concern from his cube.

'What?' I ask, before turning abruptly and making my way to the downstairs bathroom. I'm left in shock as I see my face in the mirror. There is a deep cut just above my upper lip and my left eye is black, with undertones of yellow and purple that seem to glow in the early morning sun.

'Oh fucking hell,' I whisper as yet more details of the night before come flooding back into my mind.

Felix's tight, hairless buttocks right in front of me as he scrambled to pull his ridiculous cycling shorts up over them. Reaching down to grab his snake-like hips and haul him off my wife, with her panties around her ankles and her summer dress hiked up to her waist.

I just stood there for I don't know how long going over and over it in my head. I was rooted to the spot by nothing other than sheer panic. Why had I had so much to drink? *You know why, you silly sod,* I told myself. *It was your fortieth birthday party.* If that wasn't an occasion to cut loose and wash away the stress of the past few weeks, then what was?

A strange combination of emotions was washing over me. Disbelief, rage, sickness, weakness, and the desperate tension and hope that it was all just some sort of nightmarish hallucination caused by too much whisky.

Was it real?

Erm, yes, you dolt, just take a look at your face. Either you got into a drunken fistfight or you had one heck of a fall off the deck.

I register pain in my ribs and lift up my T-shirt to see that there is a nice big bruise extending across the right side of my torso. Jesus, if I took a beating then what must I have administered in retaliation?

I have to find my wife. And I have to find that greasy, sprauncy, good-for-nothing bottom-feeder Felix. If I could see them actually in the flesh, maybe walk out into the garden to see them leisurely enjoying a strong cup of coffee in the sun then I might be able to convince myself it was all just a terrible dream.

'Daaad, can I have some breakfast?' Josh shouts from the next room. I rush back in and over to my kids. I suddenly feel the need to hug and hold them and never let go. I kneel down to Josh's eye level and say as calmly as possible, 'Yes, buddy, I just have to find Mummy quickly and Uncle Fixly and then I'll come back in and make you all some pancakes. Sound good?'

That instantly appeases my son and he goes back to concentrating on his Rubik. A tear forms in my eye as I look at him and his sister and a tidal wave of sadness sweeps over me as I realise that this might be one of the defining moments of their short lives so far. The day they found out their mummy and daddy were getting a divorce.

Of course, I still had no idea at that point that things were going to get a lot, lot worse.

13

NEVIN

Our car is out front, which means she can't have high-tailed it off to her mother's for some sort of woe-is-me solace and sympathy. But I've searched the entire house and garden top to bottom and there's no sign of Gloria anywhere. She must really be feeling guilty, and has probably gone for a walk along the clifftops or down on the beach to clear her head and try come up with some sort of explanation. Time enough for that later. There will be reprisals. I don't care how much pleading she does or what sort of defence she comes up with.

The only place I haven't looked is the scene of the crime, so to speak.

The summer house itself.

My whole body is stiff with tension as I realise that's where they must still be.

The nerve to think they could cosy up together after what they had done!

I still can't recall anything after the image of Felix pumping away on top of my wife, which is in itself disturbing to say the least. How did I get from seeing that as my last recollection to making it into my own bed, while somehow getting beaten up on the way, without remembering anything about it?

Well, it's time to get some answers now, that's for sure.

I head out into the garden where, as expected, there are a few bodies wrapped in sleeping bags lying on the canvas floor of the marquee, and amazingly a couple of people I barely know sitting around a table and laughing, still drinking from tall flutes.

'Hey buddy!' shouts a guy I think is called Phil, the father of one of Josh's playing partners from his soccer team. 'Come and join us. The morning is young!'

I ignore him completely and stride towards the hedge at the end of the garden, which separates it from the small barren patch of land beyond where the summer house is situated. Just nicely out of view enough that nobody from the party could know it was there, and the perfect place for a secret late-night tryst.

I'm going to burn that fucking thing down.

Beyond the scrubland is the coastal path followed by about ten metres of grass and a sheer twenty metre drop down to the beach below. We had to warn the kids never to cross the line of the coastal path as there wasn't even a fence put up to protect walkers from going over the edge, just signs every few metres warning that they were close to the cliff. A drop like that onto rock could easily kill you, and even if it didn't, you'd be lucky if you ever walked again.

Felix is going to be suffering a similar problem very soon.

Sure enough, I can see through the glass doors as I approach the summer house that there is at least one form prostrate on the floor inside. I wrench open the door, not knowing what the hell I'm going to do I'm so worked up, and am struck by a wave of odour that can only come from heavily sweating bodies. The summer house is like a sauna, and it only takes a few minutes of sun for it to heat up to almost unbearable levels.

'Wake up, you pair of cheating bastards,' I snarl. Then I notice there's only one person inside after all.

Felix slowly raises his head and blinks away the sleep from his eyes. He rubs his face and tries to shake himself awake. 'Oh hey buddy,' he says nonchalantly, as if seeing me towering over him on a pile of yoga mats first thing in the morning is perfectly normal. 'Great night, wasn't it? How are you feeling?'

I stand there slack-jawed at his arrogance and lack of remorse. I simply can't believe he thinks fucking my wife and passing out in a wooden shack is just par for the course in the life of Felix Van Arnhem.

'A great night?!' I shout when I finally manage to bring myself out of my torpor. 'Just what exactly was so great about it, you arrogant son of a bitch? The pastoral ambience? The endless free champagne? Or perhaps was it something to do with ending it balls deep in my wife and then punching my lights out?'

I reach down and grab him by as much of his skintight cycling jersey as I can get my fists around.

'Woah, woah buddy!' he says, bringing his hands quickly up to his face in self-defence. He licks his lips with whatever moisture he can eke out of his mouth. 'I was just... you know... it wasn't what it... I can explain if you'll just let me have a moment to wake up!'

'Explain?! What possible excuse could you have for ruining everything we have gone through for a teenage hump in the bushes?'

'It wasn't... Wait, don't!'

Somehow he manages to duck out of the way of my fist crashing towards his face. I must still be half drunk or still in shock as it just ineffectually scrapes his chin and ends up crashing into a folded deckchair leaning against the wall.

'Ow!' I scream, as a huge splinter of wood embeds itself

deep in my knuckle. The missed haymaker has also made me lose my footing, and without my balance I crash down onto a large metal crate of sports equipment. The edge scrapes a huge welt up my back, and I collapse down in a heap beside Felix, unable to staunch a fit of groaning.

We both sit there on the floor of the summer house, Felix rubbing his chin and me reeling in pain from the various injuries I have sustained in the last seven hours, which along with my hangover have suddenly made me realise I am in no fit state to unleash a furious attack of retribution on anybody.

Then, as I realise the absurdity of the situation, I start laughing.

Felix stares at me for a split second before he too starts to giggle, and before long we're both lying on our backs in a fit of uncontrolled giggling on the floor.

Finally, Felix sits up and rubs my back in consolation. 'You can stop the act now, mate, she's not here. I'm sorry about the way it panned out. But she was all over me like a rash from the moment I arrived! I had no choice! Besides, if I hadn't gone through with it, she might have suspected something was up.'

I look over at Felix and my anger abates. Jesus, this man could talk the moon out of spinning. My senses even out as my mind calms down and processes the situation.

'Do you realise how risky it was? That the whole plan could have been jeopardised if someone other than me had seen you two at it?'

'Nevin,' he says, putting on his most serious face, the one that is reserved for situations of utmost gravity in the face of accusation. 'You know you're talking to Felix Van Arnhem here, don't you? Come on, mate! I'm a pro! This is what I do. I wasn't going to let that happen.'

'It was too close, Felix. *Too* close. And what the hell were you thinking when you decided to deck me?'

'Deck you?' He looks confused. 'Mate, I bloody saved you! You went haring off down the path towards the beach like Roger Bannister on speed. When you fell over and hit your head on that rock you were about two inches from rolling over the edge of the cliff before I caught you up and pulled you back!'

'You didn't beat me up?'

'What sort of asshole do you think I am?' he says defensively. 'I carried you to bed! And anyway, your injuries have to look convincing, don't they? Or else she won't believe we got into a fight in the first place. Jesus man, I thought you'd got so pissed up you were going to blow the whole plan. What did I tell you about staying clear of the whisky?'

'So I still look like the victim here?' I say with concern. 'Because that's the most important part. She has to believe I knew nothing about this.'

'Relax Winstaaan, it's all working out perfectly,' says Felix in a mock Jamaican accent. 'You're dealing with the master here. Don't lose your rag, baby. The first part is done, but now the real fun starts!'

He gives me a hearty slap on the back and begins bracing himself by rolling his neck around full circle and taking a deep breath.

'Now, punch me again, and put your back into it this time. It has to look *convincing*...'

14

NEVIN

Ha. Had you fooled didn't I?
I bet you honestly thought I didn't know about my wife having an affair with my best mate. Of course I did. I planned the whole sordid mess. With Felix's help, that is.

You see, as captivating a woman as Gloria is, she's never happy. She's always looking for something more. Oh, she is great at *pretending* to be satisfied with her lot... the cottage, the kids, her expanding client list, but I've lived with her long enough to recognise when she gets that look in her eye that says *this just isn't enough, there must be something that we have missed, something else that we have to suffer through in order to achieve.*

I've tried to understand it. I've tried to go along with it. I believe in my own way that I have for so long that it's almost become second nature. Maybe it's some sort of imposter syndrome. That belief that nothing can ever be so great that it can't be ruined by your own actions. A form of wilful self-sabotage to make her seem the victim, and that nothing ever goes her way. And it couldn't possibly be her fault, could it? Nobody could be that unlucky, to go through life being such a good person, trying so hard, being such a conduit of love and empathy to everyone around her, that when her final goal is so tantalisingly close it remains so desperately out of reach? No, it's always somebody else's fault.

Namely mine.

She won't tell me that expressly though, oh no. It's *inferred*, and she can deny it more easily in a later argument. Subtly, and through actions so small and seemingly insignificant that you don't notice them at first. Like a frog in a pot of boiling water. Dump it straight in and it will leap out, but raise the temperature ever so slowly and it won't even notice as it boils to death.

That's what long-term emotional abuse does to someone. And I've been cooked for so long that my masculinity and my self-worth are eroded and I'm basically a shell of the man I was when we met.

I wasn't always so emotionally unavailable. At the start of our relationship I was truly carefree. Nothing in the world could faze me. And we never seemed to argue. There was nothing to argue *about*, we were just having a good time, absorbed in the early flush of love. There was nothing so serious that it couldn't be fixed with a cuddle and a few soothing words.

That was of course before we grew up a bit and started conforming to society's expectations that a young couple should inevitably get married and procreate. Then the arguments turned nastier, more stinging, and my emotional attempts to apply some cool to the heat weren't enough. On the contrary, they were held against me as unacceptable behaviour.

I was hoodwinked into believing that that was how problems got solved, not with kindness and physical comfort and attempts at understanding, but by sitting down and methodically having it pointed out how the whole issue was my fault in the first place. Any emotional reaction I may have had to that was instantly dismissed, as the real facts according to Gloria were laid bare. And so, never knowing what was and was not acceptable in her eyes, I started to temper my emotions.

Until it just became easier not to have any at all.

Gloria just loves to lecture people. She loves to assume the moral high ground on every subject and is not afraid to tell people that she knows best. Because if they do what she says, the problem will never come up again, will it?

There. Crisis solved, à la Gloria.

I even had therapy over it. Once a week I'd trot off to Bristol under the illusion of doing some research for a novel and meet with a woman named Hilary Logg. Hilary Logg slowly came to understand the problem that I had, but as with any therapist she wasn't there to offer me a solution, only to prompt me into finding one for myself. That's what I found so exasperating about it. All I wanted was for somebody to tell me what I should do. But if it was that easy then everyone would have therapy on a daily basis and there would be no need for a government or a military or anything else that's redundant in a utopian society.

And that's why the stats say one in two marriages end in divorce. Which is what I felt was my only remaining option. But how to divorce in such a way as to make it speedy, painless and, most importantly, cheap?

Unfortunately you couldn't just divorce someone willy-nilly. There has to be a reason for it. The most common was adultery. Then there was unreasonable behaviour (though Christ knew what that actually meant), desertion, or two years of agreed separation. Five years if the other party didn't agree to it.

When you're in a desperate situation you are invariably willing to resort to desperate measures to get yourself out of it. In hindsight, maybe I would have done things differently. But in the heat of the frying pan even the fire on the underside of it looks more appealing...

I just had to work out how to get my wife to have an affair and think it was all her idea. I knew it wouldn't be that hard. She's so messed up over her own relationship with her father that she seeks sexual validation from virtually every guy she meets.

Yeah, you heard that right. Gloria is incapable of spending time with a man unless she knows that he wants to sleep with her. Especially if he's a bit older. It's her extraordinary way of getting validation. It doesn't mean she will actually go ahead and sleep with him, but she has to know that the option could be there. And if it categorically isn't, she'll find something wrong with him so she can discard him. *He's creepy,* or *he's not our kind of people,* or *I think he cheats on his wife.*

She's had 'emotional affairs' in the past and when questioned she has freely admitted to that. We actually went through a trial separation about seven years ago and, I shit you not, she was all over the *first* guy that came through the door after I temporarily moved in with my parents. The gardener.

And describing it to me after we'd reconciled, she'd made it sound like she was in a real moral quandary over whether to start a relationship with him. She led him on, he showed her attention, they spent hours on the phone discussing whether it was proper to give in to their desires (he was married too, you see), and then in the end, when he decided it wasn't the right thing to do, she cast him off and focused again on trying to make our marriage work.

The gardener's wife left him.

Gloria always denied sleeping with him, and I'm not sure that I believe that, but if I brought it up I was instantly shot down and told I had no right to be upset about it because we were 'technically separated'. There was no way she would admit to being in the wrong.

So I knew it would be a matter of course to instigate a third-party affair. I just had to introduce the right guy. And who better than my old faithful confidant and best bud, Felix? I knew I could trust him with the emotional fallout, or lack thereof in his case. And what's more – I knew he'd be up for it.

But like any hastily put together plan though, there are always chinks in the armour. I hadn't thought he'd be careless enough to get her bloody pregnant.

And what neither of us could have foreseen was my wife going missing afterwards.

15

FELIX

'Mate, calm down,' I tell Nevin as he is rushing around the property like a mad dog searching for Gloria. 'You said it yourself, she's probably gone for a walk along the cliffs to clear her head and work out what to do next. You did kind of give us a scare last night. Good acting, by the way.'

Nevin is panicking, and I'm not entirely sure why. If there's one thing I've learned from getting in many a sticky situation over the years, it's that keeping a calm head is always the best option. It will rub off on those around you if you act like nothing phases you. And usually Nevin is pretty good at doing that as well. After all, he learned from the best.

Moi.

I play life like a hand of poker. I just pretend I have the shittiest hand throughout and bluff my way to victory. You can always win, even with a shitty hand. You just have to know how to read the person with the better one and make them think *they* have the dud instead.

It's the easiest thing in the world to bluff a bloke. Women are... more challenging. They are naturally more distrusting. A woman will always have a trickle of doubt in the back of her mind that a man is trying to bluff her, no matter who she is. She will prepare for it. And I'm not just talking about poker here. But a bloke, and even better, a *mate*, never thinks another bloke will cheat him. Especially not in my kind of game, where a man's honour is his absolute bond. That's how it used to work among the privileged, and not much has changed. *Need a loan? No problem, old chap, just pay me back when you can.* It's unthinkable that a man of means who borrows money from another man of means would ever welch on the agreement. Of course, that's not a page of the rule book *I* have ever adhered to...

But when we get to midday and Gloria still has not shown up, Nevin really loses his rag. He's talking about calling the police. I can't stress to him enough how bad an idea that would be. By 1pm, he's convinced that something has gone badly wrong. He's actually entertaining the idea that Gloria might have been so devastated about cheating on him that she has topped herself in shame. Ah, Nevin, you really don't know women at all, do you?

It's time I step in and do what I do best, deflect the blame a little. Otherwise this could descend into chaos, and chaos is not a state of affairs I ever like to concern myself with.

Right now, Nevin's sitting with his elbows on the kitchen table and his head in his hands, the glass of wine I poured him an hour ago untouched.

He looks up at me with despair in his dark, almost mesmerising eyes. 'She's not at her mother's where she inevitably ends up after we've had a run-in. I've been up and down the coastal path three times and there's no sign of her anywhere...'

He sounds distraught, and I'm not surprised. That's because there's only been one time when something truly went wrong for him, and guess who stepped in to get him off the hook?

'Mate, relax,' I say as reassuringly as I can. 'You know what women are like. I guarantee you she's going to come through that door in a minute with her tail between her legs looking and feeling sorry for herself. You'll have to give her a bit of a tongue-lashing, nothing *too* strong remember, and be in a grump for a few days while she does her pretty little best to make it up to you, and then you can make the next move. If I were you, I'd enjoy these next few days while you can.'

'You don't know Gloria at all,' he says, looking very worried. 'I'll bet she's already written her little speech about how this is all my fault and is just waiting for the right time to deliver it. In fact, she's probably rehearsing it right now.'

'*Exactly*,' I say, carefully retreading my previous words to make him think that was what I meant the first time. 'And she'll be dolling herself up somewhere so she looks irresistible when she gets back, gives you the puppy eyes and expects it all to be brushed under the rug and for life to go on as normal! But you hold the cards here, matey-boy, remember that. *You* hold all the cards.'

He's shaking his head in a mixture of anger and false bravado. I knew he'd come around to my way of thinking. I just had to push the right pressure points. Speaking of pressure points, my cheek hurts like holy hell after the second haymaker Nevin aimed at me. It really hit its mark.

'It's textbook Gloria!' he says in amazement. Perhaps he didn't hear my message after all. 'It's what she does every time! It won't matter that I *literally* caught her with her pants down because I guarantee you she'll have found a way to spin the whole thing to make it my responsibility.'

Perhaps a new line of attack is needed. 'Look,' I say gently. 'If you like, I'll stay here with the kids and you can go for a little run around town in the auto and see if you can spot her anywhere?'

'The kids, oh God, the *kids.*' Nevin's head falls back into his hands as he considers the implications of what this will mean for Amy and Josh.

'The kids will be fine, matey! Look, they're resilient little suckers. All kids are. Sure it will be tough on them for a bit while you work out the logistics, but they'll be back on their feet in no time. You've got to focus on *yourself* here. This is what you wanted in the first place and *nothing is fucked here, dude.* It's all going to plan!'

I borrow a line from one of my favourite film characters, Walter Sobchak, a man who had precisely the right idea about how to deal with a crisis. *Go bowling.*

'I suggest you have that glass of wine,' I say coaxingly. 'Everything looks better after a glass of Chablis.'

But Nevin stands purposefully from the table and grabs his car keys off the hook on the wall. 'You're right, I need to go looking for her. Can you keep an eye on the kids for a bit, mate?'

I'm not sure it's absolutely the best idea for him to go haring off around town given that he's probably still over the limit from last night. He might just end up working himself up into even more of a lather. But he's a stubborn son of a bitch, and I can see I'm not going to be able to persuade him to stay put any longer.

'Go, mate, go. I'll be here. We'll get the Bocce set out and have a tournament in the garden. Keep them off those bloody awful screens for a while.'

Nevin looks at me with pure gratitude in his eyes. Fine, let him go and drive around town for as long as it takes. He might be in even more of a state when he gets back but I'll be here to calm the storm as ever.

Yep, I sure am the man for a crisis. The old steadfast shoulder to cry on when times are tough.

Especially since I know he has absolutely no chance of finding Gloria.

16

FELIX

I've said it before, but I really could get used to this. The sun is out, I've got a chilled glass of Chablis in the shade of the marquee, and I'm playing Bocce ball with the kids on a sharply manicured lawn a hundred yards from a spectacular sea view.

'Now then, Josh, remember what I told you, slowly bring your arm back and aim right down the line of your swing. No, no, *under* arm, this isn't pétanque... Oh yes, my son, great roll!'

Josh skips in joy as his ball rolls to within an inch of the pallino.

'Did you see that, Uncle Fixly! I'm definitely going to win this one!'

He turns to his sister and presses his tongue into his cheek at her, letting his sibling rival know exactly who's in charge of the game.

'Now now, young master,' I say, 'never taunt your opponent. It's bad form. Your victory says all it needs to say.'

Amy huffs. 'This game is boooring. Why can't we go down to the beach?'

'You're absolutely right, monstress, I don't know how much more of a beating I can take from this young whippersnapper anyway,' I say, pointing in mock aggression at Josh. 'Why don't you go and jump into your wetsuits and we'll pop down for a little dip in the ocean-arooney.'

The kids shout 'Yay!' and bolt into the house to get ready. I take another sip of wine and gaze longingly at the ocean. The temperature should be just about perfect for a mid-afternoon dip.

'Where's Mummy and Daddy?' Josh says as he springs out in his wetsuit. 'Have they had another argument?'

'Not a bit of it, scamp,' I say. 'They've just gone to sort out a few things in town. They'll be back in a jiffy. Meanwhile, I think I heard the dulcet bells of the ice-cream truck in the distance, or am I just imagining it?'

Josh peels his ears to the sky and listens with the intent of an eleven-year-old on the hunt for sugar. 'I don't hear anything, Uncle Fixly,' he says with disappointment. 'But they have loads of ice-cream stalls down at the beach. Can we get one there? Pleeeease?'

'We could...' I say. 'But you'll never guess what. I've only gone and dropped my darned wallet on the cycle here and I'm all out of sponduliks...'

Josh looks at me in confusion for a split second before registering that I'm talking about money. 'I've got loads of money in my piggy bank!' he says with pride. 'I've been saving for my soccer trial in Madrid next summer. I've got eighty pounds!'

'Crikey O'Riley!' I gush in appreciation. 'That should cover us for about, oh... forty ice creams?'

'We can't spend it all on ice cream, Uncle Fixly!' he says. 'My dad would go apeshit.'

'Joshua Felix Campbell!' I say in faux outrage. 'Do you kiss your mother with that mouth? Okay, run and grab us a tenner like a good chap and we'll have cones all round.'

'Can I get a 99 flake too?'

'If you're good to your sister for the rest of the day, then yes.'

He rolls his eyes but relents. 'Okaaaay.'

'Right, grab a towel while you're in there and we'll get marching.'

The beach is only a two-minute walk down the coastal path at the end of the garden. The kids race ahead leaving me to stroll casually down the well-worn path contemplating a quite fabulous day so far. Treme-on-Sea has been called 'God's waiting room' thanks to its ageing population, who retire here to live out their days in the sea air and the languid, parochial way of life. I've actually found it to be quite a vibrant little town. Everywhere I look there are young families out enjoying themselves with a day at the beach. There are two fantastic schools, a couple of passable restaurants, and that bastion of middle-class retail, a Waitrose supermarket. I imagine the negative connotations about the elderly populace are only really put forward by the jealous masses who would like to live here but can't afford it.

The kids first head to the rock pools since it's low tide, and we search for crabs and molluscs. It must be the school holidays as the beach is teeming with red-shouldered children running around and trying to avoid having sun lotion lathered on them by their concerned parents. I note with appreciation that there are quite a few yummy mummies in bikinis sunning themselves on beach towels. More fodder for the Van Arnhem cannon. I grin to myself.

Wading down to the water's edge I'm just about to refresh myself with a dip in the sea to wash the night off my cycling gear, when I hear Amy shout over from a rocky outcrop that has been revealed by the low tide.

'Uncle Fixly! Come and look at this! I think I've found something.'

'Bring it here, petal, would you?' I shout back, not fancying a thirty-metre trek over burning sand in my bare feet. She runs towards me carrying something very wet. It looks like a piece of clothing.

'What have you got there, princess?' I ask, straining my eyes to get a better look at her approaching. She runs breathlessly up to me and holds the item out with questioning eyes.

'It's a dress! It's my mummy's yellow dress,' she says, at first with evident pleasure at having found it. But then she looks up at me in horror. 'It's got blood on it! Why would Mummy have left it down here on the beach?'

'Why indeed,' I say, taking the item from her and scrutinising it more closely. Sure enough, it looks exactly like the flowery summer dress Gloria was wearing at the party yesterday. And there is an unmistakeable browny-red blotch of a bloodstain.

'She must have gone for a midnight skinny dip! Perhaps she cut herself on a rock, I'm sure it's nothing serious,' I tell Amy, winking at her to infer this is the sort of secret we don't tell anybody about.

'I'll bring it back for her!' she says, ever the goody-goody.

'Wait a second, petal,' I say quickly, my brain working overtime. 'Are you absolutely sure it's hers? We don't want to deprive some poor lady of her clothes when she gets out of the sea, do we?'

'It is hers!' she says resolutely. 'Look, it's even got her little dragonfly brooch pinned to it. Mummy loves dragonflies; they are her favourite flying insect.'

Okay, no question then. I really should have seen that. I silently curse myself for not being more attentive to detail. I think for a second before deciding this may not be such a bad thing after all.

'Okay pumpkin, well why don't we enjoy our swim and

then we can take it back up to the house and stick it in the washing machine. Salt water isn't very good for clothes, you know.'

'Why not? Mummy says salt water is healing.'

'For cuts and scrapes, there's nothing better. But the salt gets into the material on clothes and makes it rot. And we wouldn't want that to happen, would we?'

'No! It's Mummy's favourite dress,' she says.

'And I'm sure she'll be delighted you found it for her. You are a good little girl, aren't you?'

Amy looks very happy with herself and runs full pelt into the water, finishing up with a dive into the sea that's less than graceful. I hope that lack of self-consciousness lasts in her well into her teenage years, but know that it will probably disappear as soon as she hits thirteen.

I contemplate burying the dress in the sand and telling her that I already whisked it back up to the house, but she's a precocious little thing. Never assume kids are stupid. They notice a hell of a lot more that we give them credit for.

So I think quietly for a few moments, as I always do, about how to turn this potential spanner in the works to my advantage. But that all goes to pot the second we top the hill on the way back to the house and I see what's waiting for us.

There's a police car in the drive.

17

NEVIN

'Run me through these events one more time please, Mr Campbell,' the officious police constable says.

We're all sitting around the kitchen table with the cups of tea Felix insisted on making us. He's brooding, I can tell. And I know it's because he's not happy that I involved the filth. But after a full hour of driving around just about every street in Treme and seeing neither hide nor hair of Gloria anywhere, I panicked and did the only thing that came to mind. I had to call the cops.

I was praying that by the time I got home I would see Gloria sitting on the steps up to the front door, ready to begin convincing me that her banging my best mate was entirely down to me, and to be honest, I would have welcomed the sight. I had already called the local police station by this point and was hoping that on arriving home I could call them straight back and declare it was all a false alarm.

Now I'm sat opposite not one but two officers in their full police regalia. The one who has done most of the talking is a tall and completely bald giant of a fellow. He looks exactly like Dwayne Johnson. The Rock. You should have seen the look on

Josh's face when he caught sight of him in his impressive uniform, complete with shoulder radio, holster of pepper spray, and boots that had been shined to such a buff you could see your face in them. That was what I was currently doing. Sitting with my head down staring at my reflection in his boots.

The other officer is female, a lot younger, with her blonde hair pulled back in a bun so tight I'm surprised she doesn't have a permanent headache. Despite her youth she still exhibits the stern air of the experienced and world-weary plod. I sip my tea and sigh in frustration.

'We had a bit of an argument last night, like I said, and nobody has seen her since. We've searched the whole house, the garden, the coastal path and the entire town. I've called her mother in Axmouth and she's not there either. I don't know what else to tell you.'

PC The Rock is busy writing on his notepad using a half-size biro, which looks ludicrously small in his enormous hands. 'And this... argument,' he says, looking up and straight at me. 'What exactly did that involve?'

I have to turn around and check that the kids are out of earshot. I've given them their iPads and told them to go to their rooms while the grown-ups talk. This was not easy to do as Josh was determined to be involved and I could see him desperate to ask The Rock all sorts of questions about his gear.

I turn to Felix, who has gone as green as a little boy forced to eat his vegetables at school.

'Uh, I think perhaps I can answer that, officer,' Felix says in his plummy drawl. He's got his hand on my shoulder and is rubbing it very lightly. I'm aware it must look slightly odd to the officers. 'It's partly my fault after all. Gloria and I have been, how can I put this, more... *involved* than we perhaps should have been of late.'

The other PC gives Felix a wilting look of disgust and

mutters, 'Mm-hmm. When you say *involved,* sir, what exactly do you mean?'

'They've been having an affair, okay?!' I blurt out far too loudly, then instantly whip round to check the kids are still in their rooms.

'That why you both look like you've gone a few rounds with Lennox Lewis, is it sir?' asks The Rock.

'Yes, okay, we may have got a little rambunctious last night after a few too many drinks, but it was my birthday, okay? And look, none of that matters, I just want to find my wife!'

'It doesn't matter that your *friend* here was involved with your wife, sir?' he asks in mock surprise. 'I have to say, if I'd found out something like that about my wife I'm not sure I'd be acting with such restraint.'

'What?' I say, getting annoyed. 'What has that got to do with anything? Look, you're supposed to be helping me find my wife, not casting about vague conjecture over someone boning *yours!*'

'I'm quite aware of my job, sir, don't you worry about that.' He pauses and takes a side glance at his partner, who is staring at Felix with distaste written all over her face.

'Look, I'm not going be judged by you people, okay? Just tell me what you're planning to do to find Gloria.'

Rock looks at me for what seems like an eternity but is in fact only a few seconds as I can hear the clock ticking on the wall in the silence.

'Well, Mr Campbell, look at it from our point of view. We show up to a potential missing persons report to find a man exhibiting some quite nasty facial injuries, who says he's rowed with his wife and been involved in an altercation with a... an acquaintance whom he's just discovered is having an affair with said wife. I don't claim to be Perry Mason, Mr Campbell, but you can see why we might be slightly suspicious of what has actually transpired, can't you?'

I look at him and it clicks. 'What? You think *I* had something to do with her going missing?!' I blurt.

'Not just you, sir,' says the female PC less than ambiguously.

'Look, I love my wife very much. There's nothing I wouldn't do for her, and Felix, well, he's my oldest mate!'

'Indeed, sir,' says the female PC, before she decides to change tack slightly. 'So your wife, uh, Gloria, has been missing since 7am this morning, is that correct?'

'Yes. No. I mean, I think so. I mean, it could have been last night that she took off after the argument,' I say, my mind spinning a hundred miles an hour.

'Did anyone see her last night after the row?' asks Rock, looking up at Felix.

'No, I don't think so, I kind of don't remember what happened after the fight,' I say, realising how bloody suspicious this all sounds.

Felix looks up from his tea and shrugs. 'No, I fell asleep, I'm afraid.'

'Where was that, sir?'

'In the summer house in the garden,' he says smoothly.

How is he remaining so calm?

'I see,' said Rock. 'Well, the procedure in these situations, sir, is that we normally wait twenty-four hours before classifying an official missing persons case. If you are able to furnish us with a recent photograph of your wife now, then we can enter it into our system and get the ball rolling at our end, should the need arise later to upgrade your wife to officially missing.'

'Can't you at least help me look for her? I mean, what else are you doing today?' I instantly sound like the kind of entitled prick you hear telling the police to 'solve some real crimes' instead of hassling them.

'I'm afraid it doesn't work like that, sir,' says the female PC.

'And I assure you we have plenty to be getting on with in the meantime.'

'Yes, of course, I'm sorry,' I say. 'It's just that we are very worried about her.'

'Of course, sir,' says Rock. 'I can say that in these circumstances the missing party usually turns up unharmed within the first twenty-four hours. Now, unless there's anything else you'd like to tell us, we'll be on our way for now.'

I look at Felix who almost imperceptibly shakes his head at me, as if to say, *Keep your bloody mouth shut, you idiot, you've done enough harm as it is.*

'What else can I tell you?' I ask. 'She's never done anything like this before. I mean, we've had arguments before, but what married couple hasn't? It's just so unlike her to disappear off the radar for so long!'

'Does she have her phone with her?' asks Rock.

'I presume so. It's not anywhere around the house, and she never leaves home without it. Christ, she never even goes to the bathroom without it,' I say, *and for the love of God did I just utter an ironic little laugh?*

'Any clothes or luggage missing?'

'No, I don't think so. I haven't checked, if I'm honest.'

'It sounds like your wife may be simply taking a few hours to absorb the gravity of the situation and clear her head,' says The Rock, which is exactly what I expected him to say. 'If she hasn't returned safe and sound by tomorrow morning then please do give us another call.'

He looks over at his partner as if to say *we're done here,* and they both rise and make for the door.

Then something happens that may very well haunt me for the rest of my days.

18

FELIX

'We found her dress.'
Oh shit.

Amy and Josh must have been listening to the whole Christing conversation. Amy pokes her head around the door of the kitchen and slowly comes in, closely followed by her brother. Oh the poor little loves, they must have been far more worried than they were letting on, or else Amy wouldn't have inserted *that* little morsel into a very grown-up conversation. I'd expressly warned them both, in the sternest terms possible without scaring them, to keep their mouths shut and let the adults sort out the situation!

But I suppose you can't blame two curious children for wanting to help find their mummy, especially when the rozzers are in their kitchen questioning their clearly distraught father. Nevin really should have been more thorough about making sure they were definitely in their rooms.

Now the cat is *really* out of the bag.

'Excuse me, miss, you found something belonging to your mother?' says the enormous PC, who looks more like he belongs in a Marvel movie than patrolling the streets of a quiet seaside town. He sends a chilling look at his partner, the stern female copper whom I doubt could be charmed into bed by Sean Connery himself.

'We found the dress she was wearing last night, down by the beach,' says Amy, worry etched across her face.

'I see,' says the action-man cop, who immediately diverts his eyes to me. Nevin is also staring at me with a probing look. 'This wasn't something you felt the need to tell us, sir?'

'Well, look,' I say, my mind desperately trying to pull a believable excuse from the recesses of my brain. 'We found an old dress on the beach, yes, but it could be anybody's. Poor little love obviously thinks it must belong to her mum,' I say, giving Amy a sympathetic look.

'It is hers!' says Amy emphatically. 'Look, it's even got her little dragonfly brooch on it.' She holds it out for all to see. 'That's why we wanted to bring it home. Uncle Fixly says he's going to wash it for her for when she gets back.'

This is bad. I close my eyes for a split second in an attempt to gather my thoughts. I've been in some scrapes before where I've had to rely on every single ounce of my nous to sound convincing and talk an accuser down. But I've never had to do it with two sceptical members of Devon and Cornwall Police.

The frigid-looking PC turns to me with accusation on her face. I lean into her and talk under my breath conspiratorially as if to stop the children hearing. 'Look, officer, the girl is obviously a little more worried about her mother than we had thought. I was simply trying to encourage her to keep a brave face on and thought that bringing that old dress home might cheer her up a bit. I really don't think it has anything to do with her mother, it's probably just a coincidence that it looks a bit like a dress she has...'

'I'm afraid that's not for you to say, sir,' she says with quiet venom in her voice. She turns to Nevin and very calmly says, 'I think perhaps we better continue this little conversation down at the station, sir, don't you? You too, Mr Van Arnhem,' she says, looking back to me.

'Now look, officer,' I begin to say, before the Incredible Hulk steps back into the kitchen from the porch and rests his hand firmly on my shoulder.

'I advise you not to say anything further at this stage, Mr Van Arnhem. You may wish to retain the services of a solicitor before we continue.'

'Wait a minute,' says Nevin with no small amount of panic in his voice. 'You're not arresting us are you? The kids!'

'Not at this stage, sir. Anything you do say to us now is being recorded though, I must warn you. However, if you don't accompany us to the station voluntarily I'm afraid we will have no choice but to arrest you.'

'You can't do that!' says Nevin, trying to keep his voice down to an acceptable level in front of his two children. 'We haven't done anything wrong!'

'Do you have someone who can come and look after the children while we sort this out?' says the female PC. I'm sure she's loving this.

'I suppose I can call their grandmother,' says Nevin, who looks like he's in shock. 'She lives in the next town along. But she might be unavailable.'

'I suggest you give her a call, sir,' says the giant. 'We'll wait outside while you make the arrangements.'

Nevin nods in supplication. I think he's realised there is very little he can do to call these dogs off, and hopefully he keeps his mouth firmly shut to avoid making the situation even worse. I am fully aware that there is no point arguing with these small-town pigs.

Gloria's mother Susan arrives around twenty minutes later

and is not shy about giving both Nevin and me a series of very accusatory death stares.

'It's just routine,' I tell her, flashing her my most reassuring smile. 'There's really nothing to worry about. We'll answer their questions and be home in an hour or two. No harm done.'

'If you'd like to get in the back of the car please, gentlemen,' says action man. 'We've radioed ahead and let them know you're coming in of your own volition. I understand a detective is on his way from the Exeter branch as we speak.'

Thankfully because we are not being arrested, *yet,* there is no need for the ignominy of handcuffs. But the two quivering kids certainly don't look reassured as they see their old man and his best mate bundled into the back of a flashing cop car.

19

NEVIN

We are finally released at around 8pm, and Felix and I cut a sorry pair of figures as we make our way through town to the beach and climb the path up to the cottage.

The interrogation was thorough. They put us in separate rooms. The detective was a hard-boiled Londoner in his late fifties who looked like Michael Douglas. He had been around the block a few times and was extremely interested in the dress, which was retained to be sent to the lab for DNA testing.

Felix had quietly warned me in the back of the police car to stick to the facts we had given at home. There was no reason for me not to, and I became worried that Felix knew more about Gloria's disappearance than he was letting on.

The detective questioned me first, probably on the advice of the two cops. They clearly knew that if a confession was coming it was more likely to come from me than the ice-cool Felix. He sharply told me to shut up at one point as I babbled and he became more frustrated with my lack of answers, banging his fists on the metal table and even leaning across it so his face was just inches from mine, his breath stinking of stale coffee and cigarettes. I thought cops only did that in Hollywood movies.

But in the end it was deemed there wasn't enough evidence at this stage to prove that we were involved in Gloria's disappearance, and the police reluctantly let us go under the proviso that we under no circumstances left Treme until she either showed up or more information came to light. I wondered if Felix had any intention of sticking to that instruction or if he was already planning to catch the first train out of here.

'What the fuck is going on, Felix?' I say as I stop and turn to him, the evening sun framing his golden hair against the backdrop of the ocean. 'What do you know that I don't?'

His face shows little sign of the tension I'm sure he is feeling. *How can he maintain such composure?*

'I know as much as you do, mate,' he says quietly, grabbing my bicep and giving it a quick squeeze. 'But I'll tell you one thing, I'm not going anywhere. I'm sticking with you until we get this mess figured out.'

And just like that, I feel a whole lot better about the situation. All it took was a few reassuring words from my best mate. I realise how starved I have been of any kind of emotional support for so long, and as we walk in silence it occurs to me how alone I've felt in the past few years.

I always thought that being married was not just about sharing your life but about having someone that you can always rely on, who you can turn to when you're overwhelmed or even just a little out of sorts. When the weight of the world is bearing down on your shoulders, a spouse should be there to help carry some of it off and make you feel like you're not in it alone. I've never had that with Gloria. But I have always known that if the shit did hit the fan there was always one person I could rely on to prop me up.

Felix.

There was a time when I felt invincible. I don't know if it's just age creeping up on me and the associated worries than come once you hit forty and realise that in all probability you are already more than halfway through your life. Grey hair, bald patches, spreading waistlines, aches and pains in places you didn't even realise could have them, child-related anxieties like making sure they're in good schools and growing into well-rounded human beings, your own parents' impending mortality. These are all things that I had never considered before I got married and became aware that there was way more to consider in the grand scheme of life than just myself.

A marriage should feel like a team. It's you and them against the rest. So why had I always felt like it was me and the rest against Gloria? I give a quiet laugh as I contemplate the illusion we had been living under.

'I'm glad you find this funny,' Felix says when he hears me. I realise he's not saying it in a sarcastic way. He is genuinely glad that I'm finding humour in these preposterous circumstances.

'How in the hell are we going to explain this to her mother?' I retort, desperation creeping into my voice.

'You leave her to me,' Felix says, patting me on the shoulder. 'If there's one thing I know how to do, it's charm women of a certain age.'

'You don't get it, do you, Felix? This isn't just something we can talk our way out of like we've done in the past. We're talking about my wife going missing. Susan's *daughter*. She must be going crazy.'

'She's always been crazy,' he says with a short laugh. 'Look, we're in a difficult spot, sure. But what does the Dalai Lama say about these situations?'

'I don't know, Felix.' I sigh. 'What does the fucking Dalai Lama say?'

'Is the problem fixable? If so, there's no point worrying about it. Is the problem *not* fixable? If so...'

'No point worrying about it,' I finish for him.

'Wise man.' He nods sagely.

'That's your philosophy? Don't fucking worry about it?'

'Just that, my man. As Walter Sobchak says, *fuck it.*'

'This isn't a Coen brothers film, Felix. This is happening to me in real life.'

'And what is real life but an extension of our dreams?'

A philosophical discussion is the last thing I need right now. What I really need is a drink. But the need to get home and see the kids and relieve Susan and be in a familiar environment while figuring out what to do next is the primary objective. We continue to trudge up the path, with me picking up the pace slightly to signify my intentions. I huff with the exertion. While Felix is in prime physical condition I am at least twenty pounds to the bad. I feel a couple of weeks of brown rice coming on, that's if I can stomach any food at all right now. Felix obviously senses my anxiety and feels an urge to bring me back into his fold.

'Remember that time we sat in The Dog And Bone in Egham and tried to drink twenty pints in a day?'

'What has that got to do with anything, Felix?'

'That's my happy place,' he says wistfully. 'Whenever shit is getting me down, that's where I go.'

'How do you not have more of a beer gut?'

'I don't *literally* go there,' he says. 'I go to the memory of it. That's what you need to find, mate. Your happy place. Somewhere you can send your mind in times of hardship. Fuck money, fuck your beautiful wife and your new car and your Waitrose membership card. Your mind is your best and worst friend. It's far more important to keep that in shape than an illusion of propriety.'

'You know what, Felix, you're right,' I say in mock wonder. 'Why didn't I think of that before?'

'Before you got married? If you recall I did warn you at the time.'

The bastard is right as well. He did warn me. He told me on my stag do that one woman and a mortgage shouldn't be a modern man's obligation. That it wasn't in our DNA to be 'shackled to a permanent aura of respectability.' If I remember correctly, I told him to grow the hell up. He'd just sniggered and said, *One day you'll understand what I'm talking about.* And I guess he was right. It only took thirteen years. I just never thought the most immature, self-involved and amoral bastard I'd ever met would be in a position to give me life lessons. Perhaps I should have listened to him at the time. Maybe I could learn a thing or two by listening to him now.

'Are you saying I should be thankful that my wife, the mother of my children, is missing and that I should embrace my new-found freedom?'

'Steady on, mate,' he said. 'I'm not totally inhuman. *Super*human maybe, but even I have a vague grasp of sentiment. But aren't you forgetting that *you* are the one who instigated this plan to be rid of your wife?'

'Rid of her obligatorily, not totally! I didn't mean I wanted her out of the picture entirely...'

'So you wanted your cake *and* to eat it, in other words?' He sucks in a sharp breath, like a mechanic looking at an overheated car bonnet on the side of the motorway. 'Life is rarely fair, my friend. You can't always get what you want, but if you try sometimes...'

'Will you stop reducing my life to series of film and song quotes please!'

'Mick Jagger is one of the most perceptive philosophers in the *game*. You'd be surprised what you can learn if you actually listen to the Stones' lyrics.'

'This is pointless,' I say, and continue trudging up the steep gradient.

Felix breaks into a trot to catch me up. 'Look mate, all I'm saying is that you need to look at this metaphysically. It might not be *exactly* what you were hoping would go down, but you can't look a gift horse in the mouth. You have been presented with an opportunity here.'

'No Felix,' I say, stopping and turning to look at him. 'I am being taught a lesson. The lesson that if you wish for bad things then don't be surprised if worse things come along.'

'To differ I beg, young Jedi,' he says. 'The lesson reads, only the hasty dream small.'

'So what, just head home and act normal and just hope that things will fall into place?'

'They already *have* fallen into place, my old cod! Open your mind to the possibilities. If Gloria turns up, then you can be rid of her according to the original plan. And if she doesn't? Well you've just saved yourself a couple of years of legal hell. And I hope you're wearing trousers with deep pockets my friend, because divorce can be an expensive business. I should know, I've caused more than a few.'

Is it possible that this proselytising babble actually makes sense?

'Gloria is her own woman, Nevin,' he says matter of factly. 'I know you think she can't make a decision without your say-so. But think about it. They're right when they say marriage requires compromise, you know. But don't make the mistake of assuming that a woman will compromise if she is in the middle of a divorce. And another thing you should know, women always like to kick downwards. And who is a divorcing woman most likely to want to kick?' He shakes his head morosely. 'Never underestimate a woman who is determined to win. Right now you're part of a team, but that will all change once that team is deconstructed and it's every man, or in this case woman, for themselves.'

I'm not entirely sure what point he is trying to make, but I'm hearing the gist of it. And I'm coming round to the idea that it may not be such a bad thing if Gloria never turns up again.

20

FELIX

The media always gets hold of a missing person story pretty quickly. They have their contacts at the police station despite how hard the brass tries to crack down on leaks. That's why I knew I really only had a day's grace before Gloria's picture was plastered all over the local papers, and then, depending on how long the disappearance went on, the national news.

Last night had been an attempt by Nevin to remain positive and calm in front of the kids while dealing with a maelstrom of personal anguish. After Susan left, we sat at the kitchen table sipping wine with Nevin keeping a constant eye on the door and the driveway to see if she would suddenly reappear, and I did my best to keep him solid and convince him that his world wasn't about to end.

I knew that once the story did hit the papers there would be a tsunami of opinion directed his way, and – depending on how much information the cops released – probably my way as well. It all came down to that damned dress. Still, there wasn't anything I could do about that now.

The next morning the kids actually sleep in pretty late, exhausted as they are from their late night at the party and the effects of worry over their missing mum. Nevin and I tried our best to make light of the situation by telling them that Mummy had just gone on a little holiday as she had been working so hard in the run-up to the party and after the house move. But like I said, kids are not stupid, and while Josh seemed content enough alternating between his iPad and his Rubik's cube, Amy was a bundle of nerves. She also could not get the dress out of her mind, and I knew we would have to keep her well away from any media speculation that a local woman had drowned after a late-night swim and all that was left were her clothes on the beach. Nothing this big had ever happened in the sleepy seaside town of Treme-on-Sea after all. Those hounds would be all over it.

I slept on the sofa in the sitting room, so I hear Nevin when he trudges into the kitchen at 7am looking like he hasn't slept in months. Somehow he still manages to pull off a kind of sexy, boho-chic charm.

'Morning mate,' I say, pulling myself off the sofa and heading into the kitchen. 'I'll get us some coffee on. Fancy an Irish?' I scold myself internally for offering him a nip of whisky in his morning beverage. I should have just put one in there without telling him.

'No, Felix. Just coffee please,' he says sternly. 'For you too. We need to keep clear heads today. If Gloria does decide to walk through that door she'll smell whisky on us from the bottom of the lane.'

'Right you are, captain,' I say, pouring myself one anyway. 'Listen, I was thinking, there's no point in both of us moping around here all day waiting for something that may not happen. There's sod-all in the house so I might pop into town and get some supplies. Anything in particular you need?'

'Yeah, good idea, mate,' he says absently, his mind clearly on more important things.

'Have you tried calling her phone again?' I suggest.

'I called it every hour, on the hour throughout the night. It's not even ringing anymore. It just goes straight to messaging.'

'She might just have switched it off? You know, sick of the sound of it while she gets her head together, that sort of thing.'

'Maybe,' he says quietly. 'Or it's finally run out of battery. Shit, why didn't she listen to me when I was trying to set up Find My Family on her phone?'

Technology has never been my strong point, but I understand that people with smartphones can bring up an app that shows them exactly where someone else is anywhere on the globe, provided they get each other's permission. 'Christ, the very thought of that makes me break into a cold sweat. Why would you voluntarily allow your wife to know where you are all the time?'

'Uh, in case one of us goes missing?' Nevin adds, unhelpfully.

'Fair point. Listen, why don't you take the kids up to Longleat Safari for the day or something? I can guard the place in case she shows up or we get a call from the rozzers?'

'Because they told us not to leave town, remember?'

'Another fair point. I just thought it might focus your minds on something else,' I say, somewhat defensively. I hand him his coffee and give him a supportive pat on the shoulder.

'It's all going to work out fine, mate, trust me. She'll have learned her lesson and will be back through those doors in no time.'

'It's the not knowing that's the worst part. I mean, maybe she did go for a late-night swim after I caught you both to clear her head, and ended up getting into trouble in the water? Or maybe she went down to the beach and somebody grabbed her and stuffed her in the back of a Transit van? Maybe she has emptied our savings account and fucked off to Costa Rica.'

'She'd never leave the kids, mate, you know that.'

'Wouldn't she? I'm honestly not convinced. She can be very single-minded when she wants something.'

'Can't we all?' I say.

'Listen, Felix, did she ever tell you anything about me when you two were, you know, "secretly" meeting?'

'Do you really want to know what we did in Hamburg?' I say, slightly surprised.

'Not *that*,' Nevin replies with mild irritation. 'I mean, did she talk about anything that might give you an idea of what's going through her head?'

'Other than what a self-centred and emotionally redundant bastard you are, you mean?'

'Felix. I'm serious.'

'So am I, mate. You know, the more she laid into you the more I realised that this whole plan was by far the best thing you could do for yourself. As far as I can see, you're either going to be the grieving husband or the penniless divorcee. Either way you're dodging a bullet. And by the way, I'm thinking about her in all this as well. Do you really think you staying together wouldn't result in about thirty more years of misery together?'

'Maybe this whole thing was a stupid pipe dream,' he says suddenly. 'Why did I think this was a good idea? I'll tell you why. Because I thought I was writing one of my stupid novels. I can't believe that, as a writer of fiction, I couldn't separate fiction from real life.'

'You're a brilliant man, Nevin,' I say, thinking if all else fails try a little flattery. 'Okay, maybe we could have gone about this differently in hindsight, but you're forgetting one crucial factor here. This shit isn't over yet. Even if Gloria does come through those doors we still have to see the original plan through.'

'Just when I thought I was out...' He shakes his head like Al Pacino. 'Just when I thought that I finally had the upper hand, *this* happens. You know, it wouldn't surprise me if she had got kidnapped. She'd be the only woman in the world who would do it out of spite.'

'Nobody's been kidnapped, Nevin. Nobody is going to die, and nobody is going to be doing anything but looking back on this in about a year and laughing.'

'Easy for you to say, mate. You can leave this shithole and swan off back to Monaco or wherever your next jolly is and never set foot in Treme again if you want.'

'That's a bit unfair, but it's true.' I nod in agreement. 'But I told you, and I mean this one hundred per cent, I'm not going to leave you high and dry here.'

'Aren't you?' Nevin looks at me and I can see how red his eyes are. How desperately imploring he is being. I catch a whiff of his cologne – Ralph Lauren Polo – and it takes me back to when we shared a house and he would stroll around in just his boxers. I almost, *almost* feel sympathy. Or at least what I assume must be sympathy. It's not really something I've ever experienced.

'Of course I'm not. Now look, I'm going to have a shower and get dressed in some of your ill-fitting clothes. Can you spot me a shirt and some shorts? I'm sick of this cycling gear and I smell like a Turkish whorehouse.'

Nevin nods and reaches for his phone. 'I suppose I better call the station and tell them to officially launch a missing persons case.'

There's no way in hell I'm going to talk him out of that, so I just nod back and head to the bathroom.

I'm going to get ship-shape and shiny, and then pay Gloria a little visit.

21

FELIX

The stroll through town makes me thirsty, so as I reach the esplanade, the long stretch of beachfront road filled with Regency hotels and bijou eateries, I keep an eye out for a good place to take a mid-morning coffee.

The Old Sea Dog is just one of those, a thin little place sandwiched between a hotel and a pub, with a small terrace outside where the good folk of Treme can sit and enjoy their gin and tonics while watching the endless paddleboarders brave the waters. Standing on an inflatable surfboard and trying not to fall in? It's amazing what some people consider fun. The parking bays all along the esplanade are filled with SUVs, the mating call of the middle-class beachgoer.

I order a double espresso and, after a moment's thought, a glass of ouzo. At least I can *pretend* I'm back in Santorini. The weather is perfect, not too hot and with a slight sea breeze that makes it perfect for a day at the seaside. I'm wearing a pair of Nevin's beach shorts and a loose-fitting, sleeveless surf shirt. Still, with my tan I can pull it off without looking too much like a dude out to catch waves on Bondai Beach.

Now, I know the more morbidly minded of you will be

assuming that I murdered Gloria. But I bet you're wondering more *why* I did it, and where I stored her body. And also why I didn't cover my tracks and get rid of her dress afterwards? I'm not perfect you know. Close, but nobody is truly flawless. And a good villain never reveals their methods.

Suffice to say that I believed Nevin's happiness would never be truly possible if Gloria was still in the picture, whatever form that picture might take. And I *am* thinking about Nevin in all this before you accuse me of being a self-serving narcissist. Actually you can call me whatever you like. People invariably do when they realise they have been taken advantage of. It's all water off a duck's back to me. I'm always gone before the excrement hits the cooling device anyway.

I knock back my espresso, chase it with the ouzo and pay with Nevin's bank card, rounding the bill up to a tenner. It's a twenty-five per cent tip, but it's not like he can't afford it.

Down the small alleyway at the side of the Sea Dog is the entrance to the flat above. The communal door which serves both the restaurant's galley and the flat is unlocked as arranged. I push it open carefully to avoid someone in the kitchen thinking there is a delivery arriving and poking their head out to investigate.

There is a thin set of stairs that doubles back on itself halfway up leading up to the entrance to the flat. I smooth back my hair and breathe deeply. Time to go to work, again.

I knock gently on the door to the flat three times and wait. After counting to ten, I do the same again.

And wait.

After a few more seconds I hear fidgeting on the other side of the door as the occupant inside fiddles with the keys on the lock. The door opens and I flash my most winning smile.

'Hello Gloria.'

22

GLORIA

'Where the hell have you been?!' I hiss at Felix as he glides past me into the flat.

'Well my dear, I could tell you that but then I'd have to kill you,' he says, affecting his Sean Connery accent.

'Quit playing games, Felix. I've been going out of my mind in here! Why weren't you here yesterday like we agreed?'

'As delighted as I am to see you, Gloria, please don't make the mistake of thinking I am in a tolerant mood,' he says sharply. 'I was dealing with your distraught husband, your even more distraught kids, and your frankly sociopathic mother.'

'Oh God, Amy and Josh must be going out of their minds... Could you not have gotten away for an hour at least to let me know how they are?'

'If only I could, Gloria. But you see, in addition to the aforementioned there was also the small matter of spending four hours in a fucking *police* station.'

'What? We said no cops! How the hell did that happen?'

'Your genius of a hubby,' he says laconically. 'Come on, you can't honestly be surprised that he lost his shit and got the filth involved?'

'It was your job to talk him out of it,' I spit. 'And anyway, you said he'd be more relieved than worried.'

'Never underestimate the human propensity for guilt, Gloria. Your husband is currently a shell of even the shell you turned him into. There was nothing I could do about it then, and certainly nothing I can do about it now.'

'But that throws the whole plan in the water, Felix!' I cry, before toning down my volume as I remember the floors in this old building are wafer thin and we are standing directly above the restaurant.

'Relax,' he coos, sidling up to me and stroking my hair back from my face. 'I've got it under control. We knew this might happen if you went "missing". It's just a stepping stone. The plan is still a hundred per cent watertight, providing we stick to it and you do exactly what I say, when I say it.'

I would punch his smug face if it wasn't so goddamn perfect. But I can't resist him. All thoughts of Amy and Josh are pushed aside as I throw myself into his arms and kiss his face and lips powerfully. He wraps his strong arms around me and we stumble backwards into the flat in a passionate embrace. It's no good. I can't resist him.

'Now?' he mumbles as my lips cover his.

'Yes, now! I want to finish what we started two nights ago before Nevin ruined it.'

We fall back onto the small sofa in the centre of the flat's open-plan living-room-cum-dining area. Felix's hands are all over my body, running up my hips, over my breasts and into my hair as he kisses me forcefully. I inhale his raw masculine scent, thinking I've never smelled just him before without his divine aftershave, the same stuff he always wears, and which I recall from that first night we met thirteen years ago. I give in to him as he rips off my dress and takes me on the carpet, thin floors be damned.

Afterwards we are lying on the thick pile of the rug in the centre of the flat, my head resting on his chest and his arms draped around my naked torso.

'Are you absolutely sure everything is going as we planned?' I ask him.

'Like a well-oiled machine, darling,' he assures me in his deep, plummy voice. He has picked up a European lilt to it thanks to his many summers sailing the Mediterranean in between cycling tours, and he sounds like a cross between Tom Hiddleston and Mads Mikkelsen. Two of my favourite actors incidentally.

'And you're completely certain Nevin doesn't suspect anything?'

'That man wouldn't suspect Jaws if it bit him on the arse.'

I slap him playfully, and he responds by grabbing my breast and squeezing it gently, which tickles me to the point of wriggling around on top of him. I gaze at this magnificent specimen of a man underneath me and wonder why I ever decided to marry his best friend instead.

No, I wasn't expecting to fall in love with Felix. Initially I just saw him as a way to get back at my husband for the years of silent psychological abuse. I knew he would be devastated when he found out I was sleeping with anyone behind his back, but it would be doubly satisfying when he found out it was his oldest and best friend.

And yes, I have considered the damage it will do to their friendship. I'm not totally cold-blooded even though Nevin may think so. But I really don't care. If Nevin gave me half as much attention as he does Felix then perhaps none of this would have happened in the first place.

There has always been an air of sexual tension between us, but since our affair started only a few weeks ago I've realised that as flirtatious and scandalous a reputation as he has, beneath

Felix's surface beats the heart of a truly passionate and loving man. A man who I have no doubt wants more than the fancy-free life he is projecting.

Oh, I know you're going to say: *Don't be so naïve, girl. Do you really think little old you can tame a wily old fox like Felix Van Arnhem?*

Yes, I do. And after the time we spent together in Hamburg, three guilt-free days where for the first twenty-four hours we didn't even leave my hotel room, I am convinced that he has found in me everything he has been looking for, for so long.

Felix will be far better off with a good woman in his life than the parade of rake-thin socialites who may stimulate his groin but do nothing for his mind or his desire for passion and romance.

In Hamburg we strolled through the Kunsthalle, saw Mendelssohn performed at the Elbphilharmonie, and did a guided cycle tour of the city which we left halfway through since Felix knew the roads better than any tour guide. We had long leisurely lunches and made love every night and every morning, with the scent of the city radiating from our skin. Things I could never do with Nevin in a million years.

I know it sounds whimsical and premature, but we're not teenagers. We're two lonely souls desperately reaching out for their equal in another. Everyone deserves a second chance, and this, I have decided, is mine. I'm not going to let anyone take it away from me.

Least of all Nevin.

Yes, I have considered the ramifications of divorce. But you know what I really want? I want Nevin to fall to his knees when I do return home and beg me to come back with open arms, to say he'll change and that it doesn't matter about the affair. But I want him to suffer a little first. And then I'm going to tell him right to his face that I'm leaving him and having Felix's baby. I know it's Felix's since Nevin didn't even come last time we had sex at our friends' party in Gloucester. He was too drunk.

I do wonder though if we might have gone too far with this whole disappearing act. I wasn't expecting it to last so long. I thought Felix would come and get me yesterday, and we could go home together and break the devastating news. Now the police are involved and Felix doesn't even seem to care! I'm terrified that I'll be arrested for wasting police time, and if it weren't for Felix's unenviable way of pacifying a fraught situation I'd be heading to the station right now to tell them 'false alarm!' But I just know Felix has it all under control.

After all, we planned it nearly to the minute in Hamburg.

It was a bit uncomfortable in the summer house while we waited for Nevin to 'discover' us. Felix had assured me it would be Nevin who would find us there and nobody else. I don't know how he managed this, but I trusted him with that job and knew he wouldn't let me down.

Unfortunately I didn't get to see the look on Nevin's face when he came in as I was underneath Felix, and he wasn't supposed to run off down the path towards the beach in a drunken panic either. He was supposed to attack Felix, who would then subdue him in a headlock in the ensuing scuffle and we'd take it from there.

So Felix and I had followed him. As Felix caught up with him, Nevin had fallen and knocked himself clean out on a rock right at the edge of the cliff. Initially I thought it was the luckiest thing ever, but when I saw the blood leaking from his mouth I stripped off my dress to stem the flow and in my panic left it lying right there on the cliff's edge.

Felix had carried Nevin back to his bed, past all the party guests who were by this stage too drunk to check if he was all right. Felix had just rolled his eyes and said, 'Poor fellow's had far too much of the sauce, I'm going to stick him in his bed.' Everyone had simply cheered and gone back to their revelry.

We tucked Felix up in bed, checking to see he was still breathing. He was, and was even emitting a small moan, so with relief I knew he wasn't dead. I quickly changed into a new dress and prepared the excuse that we had all just gone for a midnight swim in case anyone asked me why I had been in just my bra and panties while helping Felix carry Nevin.

But nobody did ask, and the rest of the night went off without a hitch. I was the perfect hostess.

As the most sensible of the party guests filtered home at around 1am leaving behind only a few drunken stragglers I checked Nevin to see he was out for the count. He should have been with the combined effects of a knock on the head and the amount of whisky Felix had plied him with. When I was satisfied there was no way he was waking up until morning I quietly made my way out of the garden and down the coastal path to the town. I let myself into the flat above The Old Sea Dog, which is owned by my friend Derek. He is not-so-secretly in love with me, and along with inadvertently telling me the key-safe combination over drinks a few days before, he had also let me know that the flat was empty following renovations and wasn't due to be rented out on Airbnb until the beginning of July.

It was perfect. All I had to do was lie low the next day and wait for Felix to come and get me when the time was right.

And now he's here. Now we can finally do what we've wanted to for so long. We can be together, and Nevin can live the rest of his days in the flat, emotionless cave he so loves

23

NEVIN

Thankfully Susan came over half an hour ago and took the kids off for the day. It took a bit of persuading, but I managed to seduce her by giving her fifty quid and telling her it would only be for a few hours while I sorted shit out with the police. She could hardly refuse. I asked her again if Gloria had been in touch and she said she'd heard nothing. I'm a bit surprised she doesn't seem more worried. But if anyone is party to the ins and outs of our marriage other than my wife and me, then it's Susan, and I can see she regards this as just another wave in the choppy seas of her daughter's melodramatic life.

If I was hoping for some sympathy though I could shove it. I'm convinced Susan has never really taken to me, despite my constant efforts to keep her daughter happy and the two beautiful grandchildren we've given her. I get the impression she thinks that I have always been punching above my weight. Susan is very looks-oriented. Beautiful people filter in and out of her life constantly due to her job as a part-time model. You'll be reading the Sunday papers and all of a sudden she'll spring out at you from the page in an advert for a stairlift brand or seniors' cruise. I often find it very hard to finish my breakfast after seeing one of those, her piercing blue eyes leaping from the glossy pages to judge me. It's funny how you can be the most thick-skinned person in the world apart from when it comes to the judgement of your in-laws.

Lorraine and Chris, our nosy next-door neighbours, had been shielded from the view of Felix and me being escorted out in the police car yesterday thanks to the large hedge that separates our properties. But they will have most certainly seen the blue and whites coming and going and taken note of our visit from the authorities, and no doubt the collective tongues of the lane are wagging overtime.

There will be some explaining to do, no doubt, especially as I've already had a journalist from the local paper on the line trying to get more information. I just said 'no comment' and put the phone down. It hasn't stopped ringing since. I unplugged the landline about five minutes ago, and now my mobile phone is ringing with unidentified numbers. How do these people get hold of your personal number? I wouldn't be surprised if everyone else who lives on the lane has been contacted for comment in the article that is sure to run in tomorrow's edition of *The Treme Chronicle*.

Such a nice, quiet couple.

But Felix will be back soon laden with supplies from his trip into town. I gave him my bank card and told him to get only the essentials like bread, milk and maybe a few ready meals so we don't have to think too much about cooking. I'm still too strung out to eat much anyway, but the kids will be hungry tonight when they get back from their stay at grandma's. Susan is rake thin and she never gives them anything but vegan crap that tastes like cardboard. Their words, not mine.

I walk around the house trying to find something to do to take my mind off Gloria. I've already had about fourteen cups of coffee and as a result my hands are shaking slightly with the caffeine spike. At least that's the reason I give myself; and not the fact that every nerve in my body is shredded with anxiety.

I make my way out into the garden and scan the mess that's left over from the party. Empty bottles litter the collapsible tables in the marquee and there are cigarette butts all over the previously perfect lawn. I think about starting a mammoth tidy-up operation, but we had paid the marquee company extra to do that for us. That's when I remember they are due to arrive just after lunch to take everything down and restore the garden to its former state.

It can't hurt to start it though and I'm not doing anything else so I grab a black bin bag from beneath the sink and go round the garden picking up fags, bits of confetti and the odd item of clothing jettisoned by sweaty dancers and forgotten at the end of the night. I find four random shoes as well, lodged in various bushes, and wonder who else might have got up to some secret shenanigans after dark. There were a few teenagers present so it wouldn't surprise me if I come across a few used condoms as well, but thankfully I don't.

The garden is deathly quiet in the mid-morning sunshine and I can hear the waves lapping the beach below. My mind returns to Gloria's dress and how it ended up down there. If she and Felix perhaps snuck away for a cheeky swim before returning to the summer house to conclude their business...

I try and remember what I saw upon discovering them. As drunk as I was I didn't recall either of them being wet. I don't suppose it matters much now. The plan went off without much of a hitch, apart from my impromptu decision to take off down the beach path, knowing that Felix would follow me and we could stage the fight that we had planned out of Gloria's sight. Felix had been adamant that he would get me in a choke hold during our 'scuffle' and I would pretend to pass out, but in the heat of the moment it just seemed more appropriate to run.

I don't remember slipping and falling onto the rock on the edge of the cliff though.

Something occurs to me and I jolt upright from bending down to pick up yet another fag butt.

I don't remember slipping and falling onto the rock.

I just remember Felix shouting behind me and chasing me, and the next thing I knew everything went black.

What if Felix had tried to *push* me over that cliff?

My mind races at the implications of that. Why would he do that?

A nasty thought occurs to me. With me out of the picture completely following a 'tragic accident' he would be free to shack up with Gloria and they could comfortably live out their lives on my book royalties. They were sure to spike following my death.

No, you're being ridiculous, I think. Felix would never do that to me. And if he'd wanted me gone, he could have just rolled me a few more feet and sent me crashing to the rocks below. Nobody would have been any the wiser.

Unless Gloria had caught up with him by that stage and the opportunity had passed?

Suddenly I see their 'affair' in a whole new light. Could Felix and Gloria be the ones who were actually plotting against *me*, rather than us against her? She was after all pregnant with his child and a long and drawn-out divorce would put unwanted strain on her health just when she needed to be as stress-free as possible.

The thought plays through my mind as I continue cleaning up. I'm alternating back and forth between it being utterly implausible and a very obvious attempt to get rid of an unwanted piece of a puzzle.

Did Felix and Gloria actually want me dead?

24

GLORIA

Yes, the thought had crossed my mind of doing away with Nevin altogether. I mean, what wife hasn't thought what it would be like to kill their husband at some point? You're lying if you say you haven't.

I don't mean in some brutal, psychopathic, Black Widow way like Mary Elizabeth Wilson or Betty Lou Beets. Although I'm sure there are women who think like that. I mean in the quiet, undetectable way that would simply mean you didn't have to put up with him anymore?

And I'm not saying that I've spent hours and hours fantasising about getting rid of Nevin, but there have been plenty of times throughout our marriage when I've had fleeting thoughts about how much easier things would be without him. I'm still in my prime; I'm still relatively young and beautiful; I'd have no problem finding a wealthy older guy to settle down with, who could become a loving stepfather to Amy and Josh.

But in the end that's all they were. Thoughts. Transitory echoes of a better life unencumbered by this emotional black hole that refers to me as 'the old ball and chain' at social functions. I mean come on, that's language you would expect from some stuffy old dullard sipping whisky in a gentleman's club, not a man who's only just hit forty. What man of Nevin's age thinks of his young and pretty wife as a hindrance?

But ultimately it always came back to the kids. I knew I couldn't leave them without their biological father, no matter how many fantasies I harboured about a loving, rich, silver fox of a second husband who would dote on them, perhaps because he didn't have any children of his own. But that didn't mean I had to remain as unhappy as I was.

There is more than one way to cross a river.

That's not to say Felix and I didn't have the conversation. I broached it in jest at first, in Hamburg, casually throwing into conversation over dinner the question of how, if we wanted to, could we get rid of Nevin permanently? Just to gauge his reaction. I told myself that if it was utter outrage I would immediately back-pedal with the old 'only joking' excuse. But if there was even a hint of him considering the prospect, then I would push it further and see how far he was potentially willing to go.

He had done what Felix always does when asked a difficult question, laughed it off with an unconvincing Hugh Grant smirk and a remark like 'if only', and I sensed it wasn't something he was willing to pursue. That was fine. As I say, there is more than one way to skin a cat.

I don't think Felix could ever be that ruthless anyway. I'm sure he doesn't have a vindictive bone in his body. He never talks about his childhood with me, but he always has a hint of pride in his voice when he talks about his father. I don't know much about him other than that he was a politician, but my mum knows who he was and apparently he was quite high in government in the 1980s. It's clear Felix was brought up with a strong masculine influence. He is a man's man, but that doesn't mean he isn't in touch with his feminine side. He can be tender and caring but also macho and forceful when you want him to be. *Wink, wink.* It makes my stomach squirmy when I think about some of the things he does to me in the bedroom. Always respectfully though, and with the understanding that a woman has certain needs and it's his job to fulfil them. No wonder he is so popular with the ladies.

But that time has passed. There will be no jetting off to St Tropez when we're finally together – not without me anyway.

I'll make sure of that.

He's making us a cup of coffee in the little galley kitchen of the flat. As we're drinking it together, looking out through the huge window that affords a panoramic view of the sea along the esplanade, I casually ask him what he's thinking.

My mother told me never to ask a man what he's thinking as you might not want to know the answer, but with Felix I know he's always completely truthful with me.

'Nothing much,' he says. 'I'm just thinking about our future life together and how we're going to explain to the kids what's going on.'

A more perfect response I could not have hoped for. I smile at him. 'I think Josh will be fine. He's sort of at the age where nothing really fazes him as long as his tummy is full and he's got a football match to look forward to. It's Amy I'm more worried about. She is at a more difficult age. She's only a year older than Josh but girls mature much earlier than boys.'

'Yes, *puberty*,' says Felix with a faux grimace. 'I don't know what it's like for girls but it certainly was an experience for me.'

'It's not so bad. More exciting than anything else. You're finally becoming a woman. It's like a whole new world of opportunities is opening up for you. Well, a whole world of boys, anyway.'

Felix turns to me and squints his gorgeous eyes, which I know means he's about to ask me a personal question. He always gets that serious look and I love that he is thinking about me and wanting to understand me better.

'When did you realise you were, you know... straight?' he asks, looking slightly embarrassed.

'You mean that I liked boys and not girls?'

'Yes, was there ever a point where you thought you might go either way?'

'If this is your attempt to coerce me into a threesome with one of your scrawny socialite friends, then you can forget it!' I say in mock anger.

'Not a bit of it! I want you all to myself.' He grins.

Good answer.

'No, I mean, do you think there's just a switch that goes off in your head suddenly that tells you that you're attracted to the opposite sex and not the same?'

'I think for some people there is. For others it's not as clear cut as that. Why, did you fancy boys at that age as well?'

'God no,' he laughs, 'I've always been straighter than William Tell's aim. I was just curious, you know. How the human mind works at that formative age. I mean, what if Josh were to come out and say he's gay or bisexual?'

'I have thought about that,' I admit. 'It wouldn't matter to me in the slightest, as long as he was happy within himself.'

'Yes, that's interesting,' he says thoughtfully. 'I always wondered what my old man would have said if I'd told him I was gay.'

'Would he have disapproved?'

'Disapproved? I suspect he would have shot me on the spot!'

'Well, things were different when we were growing up. People have learned to be a lot more tolerant since then.'

Felix has a far off look in his eyes, and I wonder whether it's really down to his father's bigotry or if there's something more going on.

'Is there something you want to tell me, Felix?' I ask, slightly worried.

He thinks for a few seconds and then gets up quickly. 'Yes. There is. I want you to take off that silly little dress and bend over the sofa for me, so I can have you one more time before we head into the unknown...'

Smiling demurely, I slowly get up from the chair and slide the shoulder straps off my dress.

25

NEVIN

Where *is* Felix? He's been gone more than two hours. He only went to the local Co-op to get a few essentials. I bet he's sitting outside a pub on the esplanade with a G and T and chatting up the barmaid. Damn, he can be frustrating. I almost want to jump in the car and go looking for him. I try calling his phone again and realise with exasperation he's left it behind, as it rings on the sofa in the living room. What kind of fool doesn't take their phone with them at a time like this? Or indeed at any time? Felix is a law unto himself. The bastard is unique.

As soon as I set my phone down, it rings again, and this time I recognise the number of the local police station. Taking a deep breath, I answer the call.

'Mr Campbell? It's Sergeant Kelliher at Treme Station. I just wanted to give you an update on the progress of our missing persons report.'

'Yes? Have you heard anything?' I ask quickly.

'It's a bit early for that yet. We're contacting all relatives and close friends to try and get a better picture of what might have happened. Does your wife have any social media accounts?'

'Yes, she uses Facebook a lot for work. And she has an Instagram account but I don't think she ever really uses that.'

'Do you happen to know her Facebook password and email address?'

I reel off the email. 'I don't know her password, but I can give you a few options. It's probably based around the kids' birthdays.'

'If you could email those to me at the office as soon as possible that would be a great help. Does your wife have any close friends nearby?'

'Not close ones, no. We only moved to the area recently. Her best friend Valerie lives in Dorset now, I think. I can give you her number, but I've already spoken to her and I'm pretty sure Gloria isn't there. Although if she was I'm not sure Valerie would tell me.'

I hear a pause on the other end of the line before he continues. 'I know we've been over this already, but understanding the reasons why someone may have gone missing is extremely important in identifying any risks or harm that person might be facing. Is there any reason you can think of, other than your wife's affair with Mr... erm, Van Arnhem? Is she vulnerable or have any mental health issues?'

'No, nothing like that.'

'Has she ever gone missing before?'

'No. I mean, she has taken off before, after we've had a disagreement, but only to her mother's in Axmouth.'

'Okay. Mr Campbell, I'm afraid I have to tell you that because of the discovery of your wife's dress on the beach we have classified this as a high-risk case. That means we will be bringing in specialist police search advisers and more than likely a Missing From Home Manager from another force. Now this doesn't impact on you in any way, but it does mean there may be some national interest once the press gets hold of it.

Unfortunately that is not preventable, but we will do everything in our power to ensure that it is handled professionally. And of course we may get to the point where we issue a public appeal for help as well, which the press will support us with.'

'I've had a number of calls from the local paper. What should I say to them?'

'I can't instruct you on that, sir, but I would strongly advise that you give them as little information as possible at this stage. For your family's benefit.'

'What are you doing in the meantime?' I ask in as non-accusatory a tone as I can manage.

'We'll be conducting investigations into financial records, telephone history, internet usage and of course, physical searches of the area.'

'Well, can I do anything to help with that?'

'The best thing you can do is stay put for now, Mr Campbell, and be easily reachable should we need to contact you. For any reason.'

'Yes, of course. Thank you, sergeant.'

I hang up, reflecting on that last comment. *For any reason.* In other words, if that reason is arresting me and charging me with Gloria's murder.

I decide against making another cup of coffee and look longingly instead at the bottle of whisky in the drinks cabinet. No, that's not the answer.

How did we get to this point? Why did I decide to go through with this unbelievably complex plan just to be able to 'win' at divorce? Because everything seems so simple without the benefit of hindsight, that's why. I haven't felt this kind of fear and anxiety since Felix and I were arrested in Russia twenty years ago.

Didn't I tell you about that?

Oh. Well, allow me to fill you in.

26

NEVIN

I spent a year living in Moscow as part of my degree course studying Russian and Politics. It's known as a 'sandwich course', the sandwich part meaning your third year is spent living in the country whose language you are studying.

My teachers assumed I would read English at university, but Russian seemed mysterious and exciting. I still didn't have a clue what I wanted to do with my life. My parents were both big fans of spy novels and there were always a few lying around the house by authors like John Le Carré and Chapman Pincher. It was a spur-of-the-moment choice, but since the Cold War had only recently ended I decided that learning Russian might come in useful in my future career. I had harboured vague ambitions of applying to MI5 and GCHQ, thanks to the richly woven and impeccably researched novels of Frederick Forsyth I was mildly obsessed with at the time.

So off I went aged almost twenty and still fairly wet behind the ears to live in Russia's enigmatic capital city. This was right around the time NATO was bombing Bosnia, and westerners of all kinds were viewed and treated with extreme scepticism and often hostility by the Russian people. I got around that by saying

I was Scottish if anyone asked me. Although Scotland isn't a traditionally 'neutral' country like Ireland or Switzerland, when it came to international relations, it didn't really matter. The important words to avoid when introducing yourself in Moscow were 'British' and 'American'.

Moscow was a fascinating dichotomy of rich versus poor. We had learned all about the corruption that penetrated every rung of Russian society and the fact that you could obtain just about anything you wanted with the all-powerful US dollar.

The rouble had crashed in the summer of '98 and the price of a loaf of bread had skyrocketed until it was more than what most families earned in a month. Therefore walking around the city with a wad of dollars stuffed in your pocket was a bad idea, but a few could go a long way.

I was amazed every time I took a hundred bucks into a bureau de change and left with more than four thousand roubles. The average monthly salary at the time was about four *hundred* roubles.

Needless to say a foreign student could live a pretty glamorous life in a city full of Western-themed nightclubs and strip joints. I explained this to Felix, who was still back at Durham grinding out his final year of study, and he didn't take much persuading to come and visit.

It wasn't as simple as packing a bag and jumping on the next flight though. There was the complicated process to present yourself at the Russian embassy in London and fill out about thirty pages of forms first. But it's amazing how resourceful Felix can be when he smells a good time and a free lunch. Within two weeks he was telling me when his flight landed and to come and meet him at Sheremetyevo Airport.

The first night I took him to the Hungry Duck, perhaps the most notoriously sleazy of the city's nightclubs to have benefited from Moscow's new-found post-Communist decadence. It was notorious for the scantily clad women who danced on the bar tops in order to entice patrons to spend more on booze. I told Felix this on the journey from the airport and he insisted on heading straight there – before heading back to the international hostel in which I was living.

I'd told him in no uncertain terms to try and blend in with the clientele, that this was not a place you wanted to stand out from the crowd, but telling Felix that was like trying to persuade Michael Jackson to play an intimate acoustic set. Out he went in his bright-red chinos, white Armani shirt and Gucci loafers. Once we got there I realised it didn't really make any difference. All the wealthy Russians were wearing the same things, and I even looked a bit of a deadbeat in my jeans and plain T-shirt.

We hooked up with an American guy called Brad who lived in the same hostel and went about partying like it was 1999. Which it was.

The next morning all three of us woke up on the floor of a high-rise flat somewhere in the most southerly section of Moscow, about as far away from the hostel as we could get within the city's boundaries. A young Russian guy in his underwear strolled in, introduced himself as Vasily and made us some awful coffee. I instinctively checked my pockets to see I still had my wallet and passport. You didn't go anywhere in Moscow without both of those items, and to my utter relief they were still there.

None of us really remembered how we had gotten there, but Brad claimed to vaguely know Vasily from his acting class so we assumed he was above board and it was actually quite gracious of him to let us all crash at his pad. But once he pulled out a bottle of vodka and poured shots topped off with a thick nut cordial, we rapidly said we had to get going and beat a swift retreat.

Out on the road we tried to get our bearings and figure out

where the hell we were and how to get back to the hostel. I wanted to take the Metro, but Felix was insistent that he hated public transport and told me to hail a cab.

In central Moscow you can stand by the side of the road, stick your hand up, and the first car that sees you will instantly stop and take you wherever you want to go in the city for a couple of dollars. There was no such thing as a functioning taxi system.

Here, on the outskirts, things must have operated slightly differently. I was still drunk from the night before, so when I stuck out my hand and tried to hail down an approaching car I was confused when it didn't stop and we were ignored. After a few more goes without success I became irritated. I was a bit drunk, starving hungry and, let's face it, very entitled. So without thinking I stepped out into the middle of the road and danced wildly, throwing my arms around my head and acting like a complete idiot in the hope of making the next car stop.

Unfortunately it was a police car.

All three of us watched in horror as its lights came on and the siren sounded. Brad, who could not have looked more American if he tried, slowly put his face in his hands and moaned, 'Dude, what have you done?'

Like I said, Russians, and especially Russian cops, were less than enamoured with privileged westerners rocking up in their country and acting like they owned the place. Two severe-looking officers casually stepped out of the car and gestured for us to step back onto the pavement. Brad, who spoke by far the most Russian, whispered to me that I should do the talking so as to hide his accent.

But they didn't even speak, they just demanded to see our papers. Brad winced as he held out his American passport. They took one look at that and pointed to the back of their car, an obligatory Lada that looked like it had been involved in more than a few chases around the streets of Moscow.

We sat in the back feeling dejected as the two *militsiya* drove us in silence to the station. They didn't say a single word during the whole trip, except one, when the one who wasn't driving looked over his shoulder at me and said, '*Spioni?*'

Spies?

I resolutely shook my head and he just grinned and turned back to face the road. At the station they took our passports, separated us and shoved us into different rooms. The walls in mine were windowless, drab grey, bare concrete, undecorated since the Cold War. I shook as I thought of the past interrogations that must have gone on inside this chamber. My mouth was desperately dry but there was no one around to ask for water.

It must have been over an hour later when the door slowly opened and a smarter-looking officer stepped in. He must have outranked the two who had picked us up, as he was in his forties and had a row of epaulettes on his shoulder. He also spoke halting English.

'Mister Camp Bell,' he said in a thick Russian accent, reading from my passport which he held in his hands. 'You are spy, yes?'

'No,' I croaked. '*Ya studyent.*' I don't know why I felt the need to show him the miniscule amount of Russian I had picked up by that point, save that I thought it might go some way to befriending him, if not impressing him.

'No, you are Serbian spy,' he said casually, never breaking eye contact.

'I'm Scottish,' I said, shaking my head. '*Ya iz Scotlandii.*' I study here. '*Russki yazuk!*' Russian language.

He produced a pack of *Papyrosy,* the ubiquitous filterless

cigarette enjoyed by most Russian men, lit one up and held out the packet to me.

'*Nyet, spasibo,*' I declined.

He drew deeply on the foul-smelling cigarette, slowly looking me up and down. He sat in silence watching me for a full minute. Then, without a word, got up and walked swiftly out of the room, slamming the door shut behind him. I wondered if Felix and Brad were suffering the same fate wherever they were in the building. I hoped to God that Felix wasn't pulling out his 'Do you know who my father is?' routine. In Moscow, that would mean precisely dick.

A further hour passed, and with the stench of the cigarette in the room my mouth felt like the inside of a cargo train in the Sahara. I was just about to get up and bang on the metal door, thinking they couldn't treat me like this even if I was a decadent capitalist pig in their eyes. But the door suddenly flew open again and a completely different *militsiya* strode in holding a gun. He was huge, with a shaved head and beady eyes that cut right through me. He rounded the table to me, cocked the pistol and slammed it right against my temple.

'*SHPION!*' he cried. '*GRYAZNYY ZAPADNYY SHPION!*'

I sat rooted to the spot unable to move in sheer terror, every muscle in my body seizing up. 'No!' I screamed. '*Nyet! Ya tolka studyent!*' No, I'm just a student!

What happened next caused me to piss myself. He let out a grunt and pulled the trigger. I froze, waiting for death to come. I remember wondering if I would see my own blood spraying over the table before everything faded to blackness. Or if I would even hear the report before my brain registered the slug tearing through it.

All I heard was a metallic click, followed by a bellowing laugh. The officer holstered the pistol and, still laughing so hard I swear he was almost crying, told me to get up and follow him.

That was easier said than done. My legs wouldn't move and the warm stain of urine was spreading across my midsection.

Eventually I gathered the reserve to stand and follow the laughing Russian cop out of the room and back to the main desk at the front of the station. And there I saw Felix and Brad, standing to attention, shaking and being presented with two bits of paper to sign by the evil-looking sergeant who had booked us in. I swear I have never been so glad to see two people in my entire life.

After that they let us go. They simply took the illegible bits of paper we had signed, showed us the door and told us to get out.

After that it wasn't hard to persuade Felix to get the Metro back to the hostel. In complete silence, and with thousand-yard stares, we made our way to the nearest underground station.

All three of us with identical piss stains down the front of our trousers.

27

NEVIN

It turned out that after the Russian cop in charge of the station had recognised his surname, Felix had been allowed to call the British Embassy. And so ironically the 'Do you know who my father is' line that I was terrified he would use in fact came to our rescue. Clearly the Russians didn't want the hassle of a diplomatic incident on their hands and released him, and us along with him. Maybe that's what happened. Or maybe they just wanted to give three green-faced foreign students a bit of a scare.

Well, mission accomplished, *tovarishch*.

Ever since, Felix has pulled that story out of the bag whenever he thinks I owe him a favour. If it weren't for him, I'd still be rotting in the basement of the Lubyanka, *et cetera, et cetera*. It's often said in jest, but always before he asks me for something. Usually money.

Whereas lawyers use their knowledge and legal expertise to con their way into getting what they want, Felix has always used his greatest asset. Charm. He'll compliment, flatter and flirt his way to wherever he needs to go. It's more than just brazen confidence he exhibits, it's a complete lack of self-doubt. A firm belief that any woman or indeed man can be bent to his will just by force of personality.

When I first met him as a teenager in our first week at Durham I was quite taken aback by it. I'd never seen anybody with such a blatant projection of self-assurance, who dominated conversations with his behaviour. I envied him for it. Yes, it helped that he was good-looking, suave and immaculately dressed, but there was something more underneath all that, a certain *je ne sais quoi* to which people of all backgrounds naturally migrated. It didn't matter if he was chatting to the binmen outside our halls of residence or a countess at a cocktail party; there would always be laughter, back-slapping and banter with the men and smoothness, sophistication and flirtation with the women.

Within five minutes of meeting him Felix could make you believe he was your best friend for life. And I suppose back then I was flattered that when it happened to me he actually considered me to be his best friend as well. Of all the people he could have chosen, it was me. I almost felt like an imposter when we were out on the town and I was in his company, watching him oil his way around every venue, even sometimes winking at me to convey his boredom as he stood chatting to yet another victim who had fallen under his spell.

I constantly questioned what made me so special as to always make him come back to me at the end of the night and in detail explain who he had manipulated and cajoled into giving him something for nothing.

Naturally I tried to be like him. I tried to flirt and chest-barrel my way into bed with as many of his offcasts as I could, purely for my own gratification, to see if I was able to do it with the ease he could. But it never quite worked that way. Any girl who I ended up with always waxed on about Felix, and invariably used me as a scratching post for advice on how they could bag him as theirs, sometimes even while they lay next to me in bed. It preyed on my confidence, ate away at it, made me think that no matter how hard I tried I would never be as triumphant or as beguiling as him.

And so naturally when it came to introducing him to Gloria all those years ago I felt great unease. What if she wanted him more than me? I had deliberately waited until I was sure my relationship with Gloria was rock solid before I exposed her to his charms. And I knew, even in the brief time we spent with him that evening in the restaurant, that when we came away Gloria was a slightly different person to when we walked in. It was almost as if a veil had been lifted from her eyes. Whereas previously she had been more reserved, more modest, more *proper*, after meeting Felix she seemed to come out of her conservative shell and started acting with a kind of gay abandon. She became more flirtatious, less self-conscious and had an aura of invulnerability about her from that moment on.

That's the effect that Felix can have on a person.

Don't get me wrong, I was the main beneficiary of her new-found allure. But it was always there in the back of my mind that it wasn't down to me, but to Felix. It's like he weaves his way deep into your soul, finds the best bits within, draws them out of you and drapes them over your physical being like a forcefield.

I often told him he should become a therapist and that if he did he could charge whatever he wanted. One session with Dr Van Arnhem and all your problems would blow away like the fine sand on the beaches of St Tropez.

He'd said why work for the veneer of a respectable qualification to con people out of money when he could do it perfectly well off his own bat? If he had followed his old man's footsteps into politics I have no doubt he would be Prime Minister by now.

All this plays on my mind as I wait for him to return. I decide I'm going to confront him. I'm going to ask him to lay all his cards on the table and tell me the truth about his affair with Gloria. Is he actually doing it to help me or is he in it simply to show that he can obtain the unobtainable yet again. His best friend's wife.

What good this will do me I have no idea. But I'm sick of the lies and the deceit, the endless one-upmanship, this unquenchable thirst to bend people to his will and make them think they're doing *him* a favour.

Or maybe I'm just being paranoid. Maybe he truly is a good friend and this whole plan really was for my benefit. Maybe he has actually reached the point in his life where he wants to give something back to the friend who has stood by him for so long and given him so much.

It's enough to drive a man crazy.

I'm just a simple chap. I only ever wanted to live a happy and carefree life with a devoted woman, raise a couple of kids and hope we didn't fuck them up too much, write books that people wanted to read, eat and sleep well, then retire in comfort and play with our grandkids.

When did life become so gut-wrenchingly complicated?

I'm not a conceited man. I realise the privilege I have but I don't flaunt it or want for much more. I know things would be a lot different if I'd been born into a slum in India or a famine in Sub-Saharan Africa. But I'm not going to make excuses for the advantages that were bestowed on me by dint of birth. I've worked hard and I deserve my success. I recognised my talents early on and while I can never say I've fulfilled my true potential in life, what man really can?

Enough of this existentialist babbling.

A real man makes things happen, and if he doesn't, he rolls with the punches and damn well makes of them what he can.

When life gives you lemons, and all that. Time to stop moping and look for the opportunity rather than bemoan what's already happened and what I can no longer control. If Gloria is really gone for good, then I will make that work to my advantage. I'm not going to be controlled or stepped on by a woman anymore. I have to be present and correct for my children. They are all that matters now.

This sudden burst of resolve shocks me. Where did it come from? Have I finally realised that I am a strong and confident man on the inside, just like the illusion I've been projecting for so long? Am I going to rise like a PHOENIX from the ash...

What's that sound?

I hear feet coming up the stone steps to the front door. Good, Felix is back *finally*. I'm going to sit him down and together we're going to plan my future. A future without the wife who has been holding me back and suppressing my emotions for so long. As God is my witness I will become the man I was supposed to be without the last thirteen years weighing on my mind.

Stop. It's *Campbell* time!

I look up to see a figure materialise in the porch, and everything I've just built myself up towards collapses in front of my eyes.

'Hello Nevin,' says Gloria. 'There's something we need to discuss...'

28

FELIX

Nevin looks like he's about to throw up. He's gone as green as I used to when confronted with a plate of soggy school asparagus. He rises slowly from the kitchen table with a look of confusion spread all over his face.

It rapidly turns to one of anger.

'Where in the *FUCK* have you been?' he screams at Gloria.

Gloria is still standing in the porch with me directly behind her. It's a small porch, and we don't fit in it at the same time. She'd told me to go in before her, but I'd convinced her it would have more of an impact if Nevin saw her first. Also, I wanted to see his reaction when she walked in.

But Nevin has a murderous look in his eyes that I don't think I've ever seen before, and so I swiftly manoeuvre myself round Gloria and into the kitchen to position myself between them. I honestly don't know how he is going to react, but if he rushes her then I should probably be in the way to prevent anything bad from happening.

'I found her wandering along the esplanade,' I say, stepping in front of Nevin and holding up my hands. 'She's going to explain everything, aren't you, Gloria?'

'Do you realise the kids have been going out of their fucking minds with worry?!' he shouts. 'We've had the *pigs* involved for Christ's sake! They think I bloody murdered you!'

'Nevin, it wasn't supposed to go down this way...' Gloria stutters.

I allow myself a slight grin at her statement, given the irony of it. This was, after all, exactly how Gloria had planned on it going down. I think she is quite taken aback by this display of raw emotion in a man she usually finds so compliant.

'Can we please just sit down and talk about this like rational human beings?' she says.

'Rational? You want me to be rational! You think running off for two days and putting your family through hell is *rational*? I didn't know if you'd been kidnapped or drowned!'

'I just needed some time to clear my head after the party!' cries Gloria. 'You know, you're not the only one who has been through hell over this.'

Nevin becomes dangerously calm. 'You know what? You're right, Gloria! I can't believe I didn't set aside my own private distress at my wife sleeping with my best friend and then disappearing, presumed dead, so that I could consider YOUR FUCKING FEELINGS.'

'It's not just about you!' she screams back at him.

'No, Gloria. It never is, that's the goddamn problem. It's always about YOU.' He assumes a sarcastic, mocking tone in an impersonation of Gloria. 'Oh my husband doesn't appreciate me, I'm so deprived of love and respect, I think I'll just sod off for forty-eight hours and get an entire police force to pay me some attention instead!'

'Don't pretend like you give a shit, Nevin!' she says with pure defiance on her face. 'I bet you enjoyed every minute of it. After all, you've had Felix all to yourself for two straight days. I did you a favour!'

'You think this is about him?' he says incredulously, rounding on me and pointing a finger right into my chest.

'Of course it is, Nevin, it's always about him! The way you behave, the way you dress, the way you try to *fuck* me, it's all a pathetic attempt to be more like Felix, who, by the way, fucks me in ways you could only dream of!'

Oh dear. That's not the best way to get your irate husband to calm down. To his credit, Nevin seems to be more concerned about getting his point across than rising to the bait.

'Gloria, you could have fucked the *milkman* for all I care. In fact, you probably would if he said "good morning" to you in the right way and looked even remotely similar to your father.'

'That's right, blame everybody else but yourself!' she shouts.

Nevin knew to expect that line, that it would all be his fault somehow, and I'm sure he's rehearsed in his mind over and over his exact response, but in the heat of the moment he's dumbstruck.

Gloria is moving towards the kettle. *Is she going to make coffee at a time like this?*

I know I'm partly responsible for the events unfolding before me, and that is what makes it all the more satisfying to watch. I'm waiting for the right time to interject and calm everyone down, but this argument has taken the kind of turn even I wouldn't have predicted and it's magnificent entertainment. I'm in the unique position of watching a man whose wife I get to bone whenever I want, take it out on her, with the knowledge that I don't even have to expect a beat-down for it, as it was his idea in the first place.

'What are we even fighting for, Nevin?' Gloria asks while pouring grounds into the cafetière. 'Why don't you just say what it is you want to say and we can all be done with it. We all know the unimpeachable Nevin Campbell has to get the last word. After all *he's* never wrong, is he?'

'Look, we're not going to get anywhere with blame-throwing and bitter accusations,' I say, sounding like John Lennon after one too many spliffs. 'I think we should all just take a break for a moment and think about what it is we want to achieve here.'

I expect Gloria to take this opportunity to lay down her law, but it's Nevin who reacts first.

'Well I know what I want to achieve. You're not going to get away with it this time, Gloria. You've pushed me down for too long. There's only so much a man can take. You want Felix? You can have him. Well done. You won. But you better get a good lawyer because I'm going to divorce you so fast it'll make your head spin.'

Gloria turns from the kettle slowly and actually manages a small smirk. 'Oh Nevin, you always think you're so clever, don't you? Always ahead of everyone else. Never outgunned, never outmanoeuvred. What makes you think I haven't already started doing just that?'

Nevin looks simultaneously stunned and outraged. '*What?*' he says with the air of a man who doesn't want to hear what's coming.

'That's right, Mr Big Shot. I went to my lawyer last week, and you should be receiving some pretty revealing paperwork very soon. Maybe even today actually.'

'You're going to divorce *me?*' he says incredulously. 'YOU are going to divorce ME?'

What happens next is so quick that even if I'd wanted to stop it I don't think I could have. Nevin finally loses his rag. Thirteen years of pent-up emotion explodes from him like a pressure cooker and he launches himself in Gloria's direction. In his rage he forgets that the kitchen table is between him and his wife and he goes sprawling over it, knocking the pot of coffee Gloria had just set on the table onto the floor. The glass cafetière shatters and hot coffee spews out, happily obeying the laws of physics and splashing all over Gloria's feet. Since she is only wearing a summer dress and flip-flops her legs are bare and she screams in pain as the boiling hot liquid covers her.

'You stupid son of a *bitch*!' she cries and bolts for the door, leaving Nevin sprawling on the table trying to get up and me looking on wide-eyed in amazement. In her panic to get outside and douse her legs with cold water from the hose by the front door, she trips over her wet flip-flops. Nevin and I look on in horror as Gloria disappears head first out of the door and tumbles down the stone steps that lead up to the porch.

We hear one blood-curdling scream before everything goes silent.

We both freeze, me in the corner of the kitchen and Nevin balancing precariously on the kitchen table, as we wait for her to continue her outburst of agony. But nothing happens.

We hear nothing.

Nevin is the first to break the standstill, pushing himself up to equilibrium and rushing for the front porch with pure panic on his face. He cries 'Gloria!' and almost slips on the tiles himself, but I grab him just in time and steady him before we both charge out of the porch and Nevin runs down the steps.

Gloria is lying in a crumpled heap at the bottom, out for the count. She must have knocked herself clean out in the fall. Nevin quickly descends the steps and goes to her, muttering, 'Gloria, no, baby, it's okay, you're going to be okay...'

But something tells me from the limp way her heads falls to the side when he takes her in his arms that she definitely won't be okay. Nevin is hugging her and crying out her name in anguish as he tries to wake her up.

'Felix! Call an ambulance!' he cries, but I just look on in pure shock.

Eventually I descend the steps and kneel down beside them

both. With shaking hands I try to feel for a pulse on Gloria's neck.

'What are you doing?!' Nevin cries. 'Call 999 now. She needs to go to hospital!'

I put my hand on his shoulders and look him right in the eyes. 'No, Nevin. She's dead.'

29

NEVIN

I can't quite believe what has just happened. Thirty seconds ago I was arguing with my wife about who would be the quickest to file divorce papers, and now she is dead.

Shock is more than just an emotional reaction to a life-changing event. It can be physically deadly. First, your blood pressure drops, reducing the flow of oxygen and nutrients to your vital organs. If the blood flow is not restored, hypoxia sets in as your body deprives your brain, heart and lungs of air. It perpetuates, and if you don't snap out of it quickly, you can die in a matter of minutes. For some reason, this is what goes through my head while I'm sitting at the bottom of the steps up to the front door of our perfect cottage by the sea, cradling my dead wife's head in my arms.

'Oh my God, Felix,' I mumble. 'What are we going to do?'

I don't know how he is able to think straight at a moment like this, but to his credit, Felix acts quickly. He stands up purposefully and paces around the front garden, his fingers pressing against his temples as his tries to figure out our next move. He stops for a second, staring at the chickens going about their business in the small run we constructed on the patch of overgrown scrubland at the end of the garden, before turning to me with intent in his voice.

'We have to move her inside,' he says. 'Right now. Get her out of sight.'

Am I hearing this correctly?

'What? No, Felix, we have to call the police, the emergency services!'

'Do we *fuck*,' he says sharply. 'Look, Nevin, I know this is going to be hard for you to hear, but we cannot let her be discovered like this. Think about it. Think about how bad this looks from our point of view.'

'I don't care how it looks!' I cry. 'My wife just *died*.'

'That's right, Nevin, you're forgetting that one very important point. She's dead. There's nothing we can do for her now. But there is plenty we can do for ourselves.'

'What are you talking about? It was an accident! She slipped on the tiles...'

Felix walks over to me with three giant strides of his long legs and kneels down so he's at my eye level. 'Do you honestly think the cops will believe that? Your wife gets discovered banging your best mate, disappears for two days and dies within five minutes of coming home? That's got First Degree Murder written all over it.'

'Not if we explain what has happened...' I say, still grabbing at straws and trying to make sense of it all.

'It won't matter *what* we explain,' he says. 'You think they'll pass this off as an accident? What, she just tripped down the stairs and miraculously broke her neck? Wake up Nevin, don't be so naïve! The cops have had you pinned for this since she went missing. I know it's hard but think about it rationally. When that dress gets back from the lab they're not just going to find Gloria's DNA. It has your blood all over it! How's that going to look in front of a jury? I'll tell you: a

Technicolour picture of a jealous husband who kills his wife in a bloody fight, beats up the best friend who he caught shagging her, and then two days later has a panic attack and tries to make it look like a tragic accident. And they've got me as a co-conspirator! I told them nothing at the station remember? How's that going to look in court? I'm just as implicated in this as you are. They'll lock us both up and throw away the key!'

Everything has happened so bloody fast that my head is spinning. I'm finding it impossible to process everything Felix has just told me.

'So what do we do? We can't just leave her out here and take off to Panama with the kids! We have to tell the cops something.'

'Do we?' he says, tilting his head and looking at me questioningly. 'What if we don't?'

'Because she's lying dead in front of the house, Felix!' I say, remembering suddenly that we have to keep our voices down so Chris and Lorraine don't hear us. '*Fuck!* The neighbours.' I pull my legs out from underneath Gloria. They've gone numb and I almost collapse as I hobble my way over to the hedge between our cottage and their bungalow on the other side. Anxiety is threatening to crush my lungs and I'm struggling to breathe until I take a surreptitious peek over the hedge and see that Chris and Lorraine's car isn't in the driveway.

Thank Christ, they must be out somewhere.

Felix is crouching down next to Gloria, sliding away the strands of hair that have fallen over her face, making her look like a grotesque mannequin that has fallen over in a shop window. He seems to be deep in thought. He stops what he is doing and slowly raises his eyes to mine.

'We have to get rid of the body,' he says with deliberate measure.

'Okay, firstly it not "the" body. It's *her* body,' I say

incredulously. 'And secondly, I don't even know where to start with how stupid that sounds.'

'Nevin, you're not thinking clearly, mate. I am. Let me explain, and please, hear me out before you dismiss this. I mean it. I don't want you to say anything until I finish, okay?'

'Okay, *talk,*' I say reluctantly.

Felix takes a deep breath, knowing that I'm not going to like what he's about to hit me with.

'We are in the unique position here of being able to get rid of Gloria completely and walk away scot-free.'

'*Fel–*'

'What did I say? Let me finish before you go off half-cocked! Think about this, right? Everyone still thinks Gloria is missing! All we have to do is put her somewhere nobody will ever find her, then run with the disappearance story that's already in motion. You can play the grieving husband, there will be an inquiry that won't prove anything other than the fact that she is missing presumed dead, and we can go on with our lives as if none of this ever happened!'

I am silent for a few seconds while I process the heinous nature of what Felix is saying.

'You're crazy,' I say finally. 'You've finally lost it, Felix. Syphilis must have finally worked its way up to your brain.'

He looks hurt, but quickly pulls himself back together. 'It might sound absurd now, mate, but think about it for a few minutes. You'll see. It's the best plan we have. It's the *only* plan we have that doesn't involve us having to look over our shoulders every time we pick up the soap for the next thirty years.'

'What about the dress, the DNA?'

'Doesn't prove anything,' he says assuredly. 'We just run with the story we've already given the filth. You and I had a bit of a barney, you hit your head and Gloria dutifully mopped up the mess before forgetting her dress. Without a body they can't prove anything.'

'Wait a minute, people have gone to jail without a body before.'

'It's almost impossible to prove, mate. They have to physically prove you did away with her before they can send you down. If it had been *her* blood on the dress, it might be a different story. But it isn't.'

'How do you know so much about this sort of thing?' I ask him in amazement.

'Let's just say I like to keep abreast of the legal system,' he replies with a conspiratorial wink. The bastard is even trying to sell me something over my wife's body.

'We don't have to decide right now,' he says, as if we have all the time in the world. 'Let's just get the body inside the garage and have a cup of tea.'

Now there's a phrase I didn't think I'd hear when I woke up this morning.

I can't believe I'm going to go along with this, but the more I think about it, the more sense Felix is making. It must be the thought of eating prison chow for the next three decades, but I move towards him, bend down, and grab Gloria's legs.

'You get her under the shoulders,' I say. 'I can't believe I'm doing this.'

'Well, you know what Zorba said?' he asks, actually beaming at me. '*The definition of being alive is to undo your belt and look for trouble.*'

30

FELIX

With difficulty we heft Gloria's body into the back of the garage and lay it out on the concrete floor. I look around, spy an old blanket and place it gently over her.

'What are you doing?' asks Nevin.

'It's respectful,' I reply. 'We can't just leave her uncovered.'

At that precise moment we hear a large vehicle lurching up the lane towards the driveway.

'Shit!' Nevin turns to me. 'The marquee people. They've come to clean up!'

'Tell them to come back another time. We're sort of in the middle of something here!' I hiss.

'They're already booked, they've come from Plymouth!'

'All right, just leave them to me. They don't need to get in the garage do they? Go out the back door and meet me in the garden.'

I stroll casually out of the garage and make directing motions with my hands as the truck reverses up the narrow driveway. Once or twice it clips the boundary hedge and I have to wave more frantically in the opposite direction. Last thing I need is the neighbour coming over and complaining about his precious hedge being damaged.

Luckily the view inside the back of the garage is obscured by a vast pile of shit: a rowing machine, various unpacked boxes and a chest of drawers that Gloria clearly never found a place for in the cottage. The van door opens and five women and a skinny bloke in overalls get out and take various bits of cleaning equipment from the rear. The skinny bloke seems to be in charge so I direct him round the side of the garage up the garden path.

'Afternoon! The boss is in the garden. Just head along the path, mate,' I say in as friendly a voice as I can muster.

Once they're out of sight I return to the garage and start thinking. Where is the best place to hide a body? How can we get her out of the garage and into the car without anyone seeing? And most importantly how can we do it all in broad daylight before Susan and the kids get back later this afternoon? It has to be before then, as rigor mortis will have set in by evening and moving a stiff body is twice as hard as a bendy one. Plus I know Nevin will utterly freak out if he has to put his kids to bed tonight knowing their mother is lying dead less than thirty feet away. There's also the risk of the cops showing up at any moment with a warrant for our arrests. If that happens it's *finito la musica* for both of us. It will only be a matter of time before the entire property is searched.

I spy what looks like a large plastic sheet folded up in the corner of the garage. *Perfect.* I lay it out as flat as I can get it and with difficulty roll Gloria over on top of it. A few folds of the corners and she's fully wrapped. Looking around for some duct tape I stumble across a metal manhole in the floor. I prise it aside and am presented with a dark hole.

I need a torch, so I run back into the house to retrieve my

phone from the sofa. I had deliberately left it there when I went out to get 'supplies' so as not to be contactable. I risk a peek out into the garden and see Nevin directing a couple of the women, pointing to the grass where there is a litter of cigarette butts and various detritus left over from the party. He seems to have it in hand. By that I mean he isn't on his knees confessing everything to the marquee bloke and begging to be taken away.

Back in the garage I get down to floor level and poke the torch and my head as far into the hole as I am prepared to without knowing what the hell is inside it. It looks to be a large empty container buried in the ground, with an indeterminate amount of groundwater resting on the bottom. It's got to be about four square metres in width and breadth, and at least a metre deep, although it's impossible to tell with the filthy water obscuring the bottom. For all I know it could be an off-channel for an underground river or something.

Sometimes the gods look down on you from above and bless you.

I quickly get to work, knowing that if Nevin comes back and sees me in the middle of shoving his dead wife into a hole that has miraculously appeared in the concrete floor of the garage there's no telling what his reaction will be.

With Gloria fully wrapped in the plastic sheeting I look around for something to weigh her down with. Unbelievably there's a link of chain resting in the corner. Fuck knows what Nevin used it for, but I wasn't going to look a gift horse in the mouth in my present situation. I pick it up and it unravels to about three metres in length. Again, perfect.

With no small amount of difficulty I lay it at Gloria's side, then tip her over on top of it and curl the link of chain once around her body. Then I tip her back the other way and repeat three or four times until she is fully trussed with plastic and chain.

I grab her as tightly as I can under her shoulders and hoist her towards the manhole. This is the point of no return, I think. Once she is in that hole we have to go through with this plan whether Nevin likes it or not.

I inch Gloria feet first (head first seems just a little too insensitive) into the hole, then let gravity take its course. Once I get her to her waist it does, and with sickening slowness she slides further into the hole. A link of chain gets caught on a small rise at the edge of the metal and she stops.

'Shit.'

I can hear somebody's footsteps coming along the path at the side of the garage, and I pray it's Nevin and not one of the cleaning ladies having forgotten something from the van. With one almighty final effort I shunt Gloria's body and it tips heavily into the tank, hitting the bottom with a large splash. A few drops of the stagnant water shoot out of the hole and up over my T-shirt. Good job its Nevin's and not one of my Armani.

I kneel down again and stick my phone torch into the hole. Gloria lies face down at the bottom, with the water only making it up about halfway so the top of her back and legs are in plain view. 'Shit,' I say again under my breath. *Would it have been too much to ask for a couple more feet of water?*

At this precise moment Nevin scuttles back into the garage, takes one look at the empty floor where his wife used to be, and looks at me in sheer astonishment.

'Where the fuck is she?' he whispers.

'In there,' I say, proudly pointing at the manhole.

'Are you out of your mind!' he says, rather too loudly. 'You put her in the old septic tank?!'

'Is that what it is?' I say, genuinely interested.

Nevin grabs my phone and gets down on all fours. 'Oh, no. No, no, *no*,' he moans. 'How are we going to get her out of there now?!'

'We're not,' I say. 'We're going to fill it in. Otherwise in a couple of weeks it's going to bring new meaning to the word *septic*.'

31

NEVIN

I'll say one thing for Felix. He was true to his word of sticking around until now. That doesn't mean I don't expect him to dust off his hands, say 'best of luck' and sod off as soon as Susan gets back with the kids. But if he does, at least it will give me some space to get my head around the fact that we've just hidden my wife's body in an empty tank in the garage.

Remember what I said about old houses and the amount of stuff needed to sort them out to bring them in line with current regulations? Thankfully the previous owner had had the foresight to connect the pipes to the municipal sewage system, thus rendering the old septic tank redundant. Otherwise not only would Gloria be spending the rest of time in a hole in the ground, but she would have a constant stream of excrement pouring over her. Not even her worst enemy would wish that. It would also mean unending anxiety for me every couple of years when it came to emptying out the tank.

But it did mean we had to get that hole filled in as soon as humanly possible or we simply wouldn't be able to go into the garage at all. Not only that, but with the prevailing winds coming off the sea I was pretty sure the resulting smell would filter directly into Chris and Lorraine's garden, and wouldn't that be a fine way to ruin their evening gin and tonic for the next few months?

I don't think they were too enamoured with our move next door in the first place. Lorraine had told me on a few occasions that they had moved to Treme for a quiet retirement, but that it was nice to have a couple of kids running around next door so long as they kept the volume down. It was a thinly veiled way of telling us to keep our kids in line or risk the delicate balance of neighbourly goodwill. And that was in between comments about too many immigrants taking over the town and how Brexit was the best thing to happen to the country since Margaret Thatcher closed the mines. That's what you get for moving to a town where the *Daily Mail* outsold all other newspapers by a ratio of ten to one.

Two hours later I'm still torn over whether Felix's plan is the best course of action. Part of me wishes he would just go so I could think more clearly. I know that while he is here he's going to hold the kind of sway over me that he seems to hold over everyone else. I wish that I hadn't caved into his scheme, and I know that if I were able to think as quickly on my feet as him then I would have come up with a less devious plan.

But we are where we are. There's no point crying over spilled milk. Or coffee in this instance. It's too late to turn back now. Even if I wanted to, it's too late to climb into that tank and somehow pull Gloria out on my own, because forensic examination will determine she's been dead for a while. Not to mention covered in a layer of shit. There's no way I could get her out of the tank, into a bath, wash her off and reposition her at the foot of the stairs without it looking blatantly staged.

Damn it, why did I listen to Felix in the first place?

I should have gone with my gut and called the police on the spot. I could have made it look like the accident it was. Maybe that's what Felix was counting on. He knew that once we put her in that tank there was no reneging on the plan.

Why did those marquee people have to turn up when they did!

I realise that if Gloria is ever discovered I am going to look like the worst kind of monster. I mean, Fred West levels of deviance. I have no choice but to run with it now, and I know there are going to be some uncomfortable days ahead as I am forced to play the grieving husband. Christ, what if they get the kids involved in some kind of tearful plea for her to return home safe and sound? That's something I am going to have to insist on not happening. There's no way I'd be able to hold it together if Amy and Josh are appealing for her to return.

One thing is for sure, I'm going to have to give the performance of my life. And I'm not going to be able to do it unless Felix is beside me.

32

FELIX

Nevin is a bag of nerves. I was counting on him being a little more heroic in the face of adversity. After all, he's got what he wanted. His wife is out of the picture. Granted, it wasn't exactly the *way* he was planning, but beggars can't be choosers. What they can do is suck it up and learn to grasp an opportunity. That's a tenet of life that I've always abided by.

Gloria's accident was by far the most fortuitous stroke of luck that could have happened. For me as well as Nevin. Nobody can cross-examine a dead person, after all. Nevin will never know or find out her side of the story. I can spin it exactly as I see fit.

But my main concern right now is stopping him from falling apart at the seams. It's going to take a great deal of focus on both our parts if we are to get through the next few days intact. And the first thing we need to do is get that damn tank filled in.

I've been on the phone for the last two hours calling around every merchant building supplier in a twenty mile radius, pretending to be Nevin, and trying to arrange consignment of a truck full of concrete. By explaining that we have an emergency on our hands and are willing to pay handsomely over the asking price I've managed to arrange a delivery first thing tomorrow morning. I had to use every inch of my guile and charm to persuade them that the tank was on the verge of collapse and was at risk of undermining the foundations of the building. I have no idea if that's even plausible, but it seemed to impress upon them a sense of urgency and I'm fairly sure they bought it.

All I have to do is keep Nevin solid for one more evening.

I see Susan's car coming up the lane towards the house. *Great, here comes the next problem.* The kids leap out of her car and immediately run into the garden to jump on their trampoline.

'Susan! You look radiant. You might very well be the reason for global warming,' I say, kissing her once on each cheek, and again for good measure.

'Felix,' she says in a suspicious tone. I instantly get a feeling that she knows something about the affair. Gloria assured me she didn't mention anything to her mother, but I never take a woman's vow of secrecy seriously.

'I don't suppose you've heard anything, have you?' I say with a tone of concern.

'The police have been very thorough so far,' she says haughtily. 'I'm sure we'll be hearing good news imminently.'

I'm not sure what she means by good news – with her that could either mean that her daughter turns up safe and sound or that someone is swiftly arrested and dealt with. I have to admire Susan. She's almost as self-assured as I am.

'And where is Nevin?'

The way she overpronounces *Nevin* with a mixture of curiosity and disdain leaves me in no doubt who she believes is responsible for Gloria's predicament.

'He's having a bit of a lie down,' I say sympathetically. 'This whole thing is really taking it out of him.'

'Yes, I'm sure,' she says in the same tone. 'It's important he stays strong of course, for the children.'

'We must all endeavour to take a leaf out of your book,' I say flatteringly. 'If only we all possessed such calmness and unflappability.'

I'm sure she sees straight through me, as she gives me a long look up and down my entire body and turns back to her car.

'Do let me know if I can be of further help,' she says, almost flirtatiously looking back over her shoulder at me. Then adds, 'With the children. I do so love their company. Robin is away on an antiques buying expedition so I am on my lonesome until tomorrow.'

'Will do, Susan. And thank you. Nevin is truly grateful for your continued support.'

She mumbles something in agreement which I don't quite catch and is back in her car before I can say anything further. She keeps her eyes trained on me even as she reverses out of the driveway. That woman gives me the yips.

I really hope she doesn't turn into another loose end I have to tie up.

I head back into the cottage and observe Nevin skulking down the stairs to go out and greet the kids. With my immediate task out of the way I suggest to him that we head into town for a slap-up supper.

'I don't think I can eat anything, mate,' Nevin says, looking very discouraged.

'Come on, me old halibut, it'll do you good. A change of scenery. A breath of that fabulous sea air... It's no good lying around here moping. As my old man used to say, 'Goggles on, chocks away, last one back's a wet sock, hooray!"

Nevin smiles half-heartedly and nods. 'Fine, it'll keep the kids occupied for an hour or two before bed.'

'That's the spirit! Nothing wrong with us having a couple of sharpeners either. I feel like a Long Island iced tea…'

The kids run ahead on the walk down the hill into town, with the promise that they'll stay off the beach which is now almost completely covered by high tide.

Nevin turns to me, deep apprehension etched all over his brow. 'Are you sure we're doing the right thing, Felix?'

'I've never done the right thing in my life.' I chuckle. 'That's what makes it so appealing.'

'I can't help thinking we're digging ourselves a grave here, so to speak.'

'The only grave we've dug is the one that needed to be,' I say seriously. 'And as soon as that is filled in, first thing tomorrow morning I might add, your problems will dry up faster than that concrete.'

'My problem?' he baulks. 'It's *our* problem, Felix!'

'Slip of the tongue, my old halibut. Our problem indeed. Now look, if I didn't think I had it all under control you'd be the first to know.'

'There's still time to go to the cops and tell them this was all just a terrible accident.'

'Nevin, I've explained this. Nobody would believe you. Or me. We've got to see this through, or I promise you we're going to spend the rest of our naturals avoiding gang rape in the showers at Belmarsh. And I happen to value my arse. It's one of my best assets.'

'How can you joke at a time like this?' he says incredulously.

'Belmarsh is no joke, Nevin, believe me. A couple of public school pansies like us wouldn't last five minutes. We'd be buggered and shivved before breakfast.'

I should perhaps tone down the imagery a little.

'Look, it's all cushty, okay? By 9am tomorrow this will all feel like a bad dream, and all we have to do is put on a brave face, look like you're searching for Gloria and let the magic healing of time do its work.'

'It's easy for you to say! You don't have to live next door to a corpse for the next few decades.'

'There's nothing stopping you from moving. No one is going to blame you if in a year or so you decide to uproot and head somewhere where there aren't so many memories. I might even come with you. Might I suggest Nice or Cannes? The women there can bend you in half the way they walk by.'

'Jesus, Felix! My wife hasn't even been dead for four hours and you're already thinking about your next slice of pie!'

'I'm simply looking for the positives in the situation. You've got to stop dwelling on what we can't change and focus on what we can do to *benefit*.'

'I'm not happy about this,' he says. 'Let it be known now that I am not comfortable with what we've done.'

'Noted. I've noted that down for when in a year's time we are sipping Arak Attacks in Bali and fending off cocktail girls.'

Nevin finally cracks a smile. Perhaps the thought of that was enough to penetrate the shroud of guilt. 'You know, Felix, if I didn't know better I'd say you'd planned this whole thing.'

'Don't be ridiculous, old pike. I may be a morally bankrupt, chauvinist cad, but I'm not *that* clever.'

33
———

NEVIN

We locate the kids at the far end of the esplanade petting an old man's dog and call them back. They instantly come running and ask me if we can get a puppy.

'Maybe next year,' I say off-handedly. 'Now where do you want to eat?'

We're standing directly outside The Old Sea Dog restaurant. I sort of know the owner Derek. He's a bit of an eccentric and I'm fairly sure he wants to get into Gloria's pants. She's told me on occasion how flirtatious he is with her, no doubt trying to get a rise out of me.

I realise with relief I'm still thinking about my wife in the present tense. I need to make sure I keep that up if I'm not to arouse suspicion. One slip of the tongue and the cops will be all over me. I saw in some real crime series on Netflix that the first thing the cops look for in missing persons cases is anyone who refers to the 'missee' in the past tense. A sure sign that they know that someone is never coming back...

'Can we get mussels and chips from Derek?' Amy says. 'Fran might be there!'

She is referring to Derek's daughter Fran who happens to be

in the same year as her at school. I'm hoping Derek isn't there, as I just know he'll come over and ask me about Gloria and where she is. But if I'm to maintain the image of a grieving husband in this town there are going to be plenty of situations when I run into someone I vaguely know, and this might be good practice.

'Sure we can,' I say.

'Uh, Nev, I'm not sure I like the look of this place,' Felix says with uncertainty. 'Why don't we head to that pub on the end? It looks a bit busier, food's probably better?'

'No! I want to get mussels and chips from Derek,' Amy whines.

I scrutinise Felix. I wonder if there's some reason he specifically doesn't want to go into The Old Sea Dog. But two gin and tonics later and he's perked up significantly. Sure enough, Derek spies us and comes over holding a bottle of white wine.

'Nevin! You have to try this, it's a Brut from the Severn Valley. It'll knock your socks off,' he says enthusiastically.

'Pour away, mein Herr!' Felix exclaims a little too loudly.

'Where's your lovely wife?' says Derek, looking around as if he expects her to waltz out of the bathroom.

'Oh, she's feeling a bit rough after my birthday party,' I say nonchalantly.

'No she isn't, she's gone on holiday,' Josh pipes up from the small end of the table.

'Oh, yes, I mean she's just visiting her friend in Dorset for the day,' I blurt. 'Everything's been pretty full-on.'

'Heck of a party,' Derek says. 'I could only drop in for a swift half as I had to get back down here, we were fully booked you see. I did tell Gloria at the time as I didn't see yourself. Hey, no wonder Gloria needed a fresh bed to sleep in after *that* night!' Derek winks at me.

'What do you mean?' I say, wondering what he's on about.

'I mean your place must have been packed out with guests. No wonder she needed to escape for a bit. I presume that's why she crashed in the flat?' Derek nods upwards at the ceiling to indicate that he's talking about the flat I know he rents out above the restaurant.

'She what?' I say, confused. 'She was in your flat?'

Felix immediately butts into the conversation. 'Oh! You know what? I think I'm going to have the lemon sole!' he says. He stands abruptly and sticks out his hand for Derek to shake.

'I don't think we've been introduced,' he says cheerfully. 'Derek, is it? Felix Van Arnhem. Pleased to meet you. I'm Nevin's oldest friend, from our student days.'

Derek looks slightly taken aback but takes Felix's hand in his and gives it a perfunctory shake. 'Are you now?' he says. 'Yes, I thought I'd seen you before.'

'Nope!' Felix replies quickly. 'It's my first time in your delightful little town. Now, do you do a kid's portion of mussels and chips? There's two little scamps here who've been jonesing for them all day.'

'Sure, I can do that,' says Derek without taking his gaze off of Felix.

'Wait a minute, Derek,' I say. 'You said Gloria was in your flat after my party?'

'Certainly was. Did she not mention it? I told her you were welcome to use it the other day if you had an overspill at the party. Even gave her the key-safe code. It's a bit of a mess up there with the renovations. I've only just had the security cameras installed.'

At that, he gives Felix another odd look. Felix has gone green again. He looks like he does when his mind is going a hundred miles an hour to find an excuse for something.

'Uh, Derek, might I have a quick word with you?' he says, taking Derek by the arm and leading him away from the table.

'I've just remembered, there's a little something I'm working on that I think you might be able to help me with.'

Derek allows himself to be led away while I sit staring at the both of them leaving, in stunned silence. *Gloria was in his flat the whole time.* She must have used Derek to arrange a little cubby-hole she could escape to if the need arose. And why was Felix acting so suspiciously, whisking Derek away before I could quiz him further?

'Daaad, I'm hungry,' says Josh.

I give him one of the bread rolls in the basket on the table. 'Here, eat this until the food arrives.'

Something is not right about this.

I suspect Felix knows something he's not letting on.

34

FELIX

This Derek chap was not supposed to know Gloria was staying in the flat, and this could present a problem for me. He's looking at me suspiciously. I couldn't think of anything to do but get him away from the table fast before he let Nevin in on our little secret.

Gloria had assured me Derek wouldn't find out that she had snuck in, but neither she nor I were counting on the sneaky bastard having installed a security camera on the premises.

Now that I have him away from Nevin, I have to think fast of some way to ensure he keeps this nugget of information to himself.

'Listen, old chap,' I say, whispering to him in the corner of the restaurant I've led him away to. 'I'm thinking of moving down this way a little more permanently and I wondered if we might be able to come to some arrangement on renting your delightful little bolthole upstairs?'

'Liked it, did you?' he says conspiratorially. 'I'm not surprised after your little tour of it yesterday.'

'You must be mistaken, dear chap, I've not yet had the pleasure of it internally.'

He looks at me as if I have two heads. 'You must think I was born yesterday, mate. You do realise there's a security camera in the hallway, right?'

I realise there's little point in lying any further. He's got me bang to rights and he knows it. What I'm not sure of is exactly what he plans to do with this information. I give a subtle little laugh and wink at him.

'Listen, Derek, me old mucker, you and I are clearly men of the world. I don't think I need to spell it out to you, do I?'

He raises his eyebrows at me knowledgeably.

'You see, the thing is,' I go on, 'I'm afraid it would cause the most awful stink if Nevin were to find out. I don't suppose there's a way we can come to some arrangement that would keep that tiny little fact from coming to light?'

'Well, Felix, me old banana split, why don't you make me an offer?' he says, mocking my plummy accent.

'I see, it's to be like that is it?'

'Look, mate, I don't care if you take the Queen of Denmark up there for a one-on-one. But you can't expect me to provide a service if I'm not being suitably compensated, can you?'

'Is it money you want?'

He looks at me carefully, and I can see he is choosing his next words wisely. 'I didn't necessarily mean, uh, financial compensation...'

'Well what *is* it you want then, if not money? Which, by the way, I am in no position to give you right now.'

'I don't want your money, mate,' he says, smiling at me. 'I want Gloria.'

'Excuse me?'

'Look, as you say, mate, we're "men of the world". But why should you get to take another man's wife up to my little pied-à-terre if I can't? She's clearly gagging for it, I mean, look at that drink of piss she's married to. If you two want to keep using the flat, then we need to... work out a system. Know what I mean?'

Perhaps I underestimated this wily little sod. Clearly he's not as parochially minded as his customers. I clear my throat. 'If I can arrange something – and I'm not saying I can – you would be happy to keep shtum about my visit here yesterday?'

'You get Gloria to meet me here tonight at eleven. Tell her to wear something tight with not too many buttons, and we'll take it from there, eh?'

I have to smile at the sheer bravado of this small-town restaurateur. 'I read you loud and clear, captain. Eleven on the PM it is.' I give him a conspiratorial pat on the back.

'Now, about the food bill. I'm afraid I am a little low on funds at present, but I shall gladly pay you on Tuesday, if you get my drift?'

'Mussels all round, on the house.' He winks at me.

'There's a good chap. And your little spy-cam? Discretion is in *both* our interests, as I'm sure you'll appreciate. We can't have any recorded evidence finding its way into the wrong hands, can we?'

He grins at me, clearly realising he has underestimated my desire to cover all the tracks. 'It's display only, matey. It doesn't actually record. You think I want my missus stumbling across something like this on a hard drive somewhere?'

'Quite.' I wink. 'Mum's the word and all that. Now, I'm going to rejoin my table and Nevin is going to insist on pressing you for more information, at which point you'll make up some excuse about having got your wires crossed, am I clear?'

'You'll be renting the flat for a minimum of six months, I take it?' he says, knowing he has me backed into a corner.

'Why don't we have a chat about that tomorrow?' I say. 'Give you time to draw up the paperwork.'

'Gotcha, nice doing business with you, *Lord Van Arnhem.*'

With that, he makes for the kitchen, and I realise I've got a little more planning to do.

35

FELIX

After dinner we head out onto the beach to let the kids have a splash around while we digest our dinner. As expected, Nevin collars me as soon as they're out of earshot.

'What are you not telling me, Felix? Did you know Gloria was going to run off and hide in that flat?'

During dinner I'd gone over in my mind the ramifications of Nevin's potential discovery that I was in the flat with Gloria. I can see how it must have looked from his point of view. I decide there's no point in lying to him anymore, as the obstacles were mounting up and I couldn't risk blurting out something I shouldn't further down the line and giving the game away.

'Okay look, Nevin. I was going to tell you this afterwards but I guess there's no harm in you knowing now anyway.'

'Afterwards? After *what?*' he says, looking like a man who's been gut-punched.

'When the time was right,' I say. 'Look, I want you to know that I was only thinking of you. But it's true I may have used some unorthodox moves in order to ensure that the plan went off without a hitch.'

'You *were* up there with her, weren't you? All that time I

was at home shitting myself and you knew exactly where Gloria was!'

'Yes, okay, that's true,' I say carefully, 'but like I said, I had it all carefully planned out. I couldn't risk telling you where she was because I thought you might lose it. I had to make sure you had plausible deniability if the cops got involved! Which, by the way is precisely what happened...'

'And Derek saw you with her?'

'No!'

'Felix...'

'Okay, yes, he did. But he's not going to *say* anything. I worked it out with him.'

'What do you mean? How can you be sure he's not going to spill his guts as soon as he sees her picture on the front pages tomorrow morning?'

'Will you stop worrying, Nevin? I've got it under control...'

'No, Felix! You don't have anything under control! It's all slipping away from us! Oh God, I knew we should have come clean to the cops.'

'Nothing is fucked here, dude. I just need you to *trust* me on this one.'

'Trust you? You've been lying to me the whole time!'

'For your own benefit!' I say exasperatedly.

'What did you say to Derek?'

'Like I said, I've made an arrangement with him.'

'What kind of arrangement? Are you paying him? Because I can assure you, Felix, no amount of money is going to keep him quiet when he discovers Gloria has gone missing. He's going to go straight to the filth and tell them what he knows. And then what?'

I choose my next words carefully. I pretend to think for a second, then turn to Nevin and nod my head decisively. 'You're right. Perhaps we can't trust him,' I say.

'So what are we going to *do*?'

'Will you be quiet for a second and let me think?'

Nevin throws his arms in the air in frustration and walks off down the beach. That little exchange went off without a hitch.

Unfortunately for Derek, his usefulness has run its course.

36

NEVIN

For the second time in two days I'm shaken awake, not this time by the small hands of my daughter but by the firm, rough ones of Felix. It's still dark and I'm very woozy, as though I had way too much to drink the night before.

'What time is it?' I croak.

'Need you to wake up I'm afraid, old trout.'

I glance at the alarm clock beside the bed. 'It's 3am. Are you out of your mind?'

'Got a bit of a job that requires your assistance.'

I sit up, running my hands over my face briskly to shake off the sleep. At first I don't see Felix, only hear him, but I can feel he's sat on the edge of my bed. As my eyes slowly adjust to the darkness I can just make out his face by the light of the alarm. Everything below that is black, giving him the appearance of a floating head. I instantly assume I must be dreaming, before I feel a hard pinch on my arm.

'Ow!' I let out a small shriek of pain.

'Shhh. You'll wake the kids,' he whispers.

'What the fuck is going on, Felix?' I say, now fully awake.

'Don't say anything, just follow me. Now.'

He stands and makes his way out of the bedroom and I hear him quietly descending the stairs.

What kind of half-baked idea has he got into his head now? I pull on some shorts over my boxers and throw on a T-shirt.

The cottage is dark and quiet, as you would expect in the middle of the night. I realise that because I am a heavy sleeper I've never seen it at this time of the night. There is a ghostly hue to the yellow walls of the staircase. They almost seem to wobble slightly as if the cottage took on a life of its own in the middle of the night. I don't normally feel this way when I wake up, even after three whiskies before bed.

Felix is waiting for me in the kitchen, fully dressed in black from head to toe.

'What the fuck is going on, Felix?' I whisper.

'Where are your car keys?'

'Hanging up on the wall where they always are. Why?'

'Get them and come down to the car now.'

'Felix, I'm not going anywhere until you tell me what the hell is going on.'

'Just *trust* me. I need you to come with me now. There's been a slight change of plan.'

'What plan?' I say in confusion.

'Never mind that now, just get your shit together and come out to the car. Don't wear any shoes.'

'Don't wear shoes? What are you on about?'

'Bare feet, that's important.'

Before I can quiz him further he's out of the porch and into the night. I shake my head in disbelief before I grab the car keys off the wall and follow him outside. The night air hangs heavy for this time of year, and sweat is forming under my arms already.

Felix is pointing to the car. 'Unlock it. Use the keys, not the fob.'

'I can't leave the kids on their own!'

'We'll only be gone five minutes,' he says, waving his hand in dismissal. 'Come on, get a move on.'

I walk slowly past the garage. Although the door is firmly shut, and locked, I can't help shivering as I think about what's inside. I unlock the car with the key, rather than using the automatic sensor which would make the lights flash on and off a few times. Whatever we're doing out here, Felix obviously wants it to be secret.

'Get in. The light will be coming up soon,' he says, climbing into the passenger-side seat.

'Where are we going?' I say, sitting in the driver seat.

'Just drive and follow my directions.'

His tone is one of finality, and I realise it's simply not worth questioning him further on this matter. The quicker I take him wherever the hell he wants to go, the sooner I can get back into bed and resume my much-needed sleep.

'Don't start it, just ease off the handbrake and let it roll. No lights.'

The driveway is on a slight downward gradient, so I ease off the brake and the car slowly rolls down towards the lane. I have to grip the wheel tightly as the power steering hasn't come on yet with the ignition.

We roll the car about a hundred metres until we get to the end of the lane, where it meets the main road that leads up the steep hill to our cottage. Felix is watching the road carefully, checking to make sure there are no other cars around.

'Okay, start it now, quietly.'

'You can't start a car quietly, Felix. What do you want me to do, tell it to shut up?'

'Just start it!'

I do as he tells me, and as the lights automatically come on I can finally see roughly where I'm headed.

'Where are we going?' I ask in confusion.

'Just head towards the esplanade.'

We drive on, the silence of the morning sounding very strange in my ears. At the bottom of the hill I turn the car left and we drive through the small ford of water that runs through town and leads down to the sea. The water splashes up the side of the car and Felix takes a sharp intake of breath at the noise it makes.

'Slower!' he whispers.

I inch the car through the water and we continue out of the other side, until we see the street lights running along the esplanade.

'Okay, now where?'

'Take us outside The Old Sea Dog,' he says, still glancing all around him.

'What? Now is hardly the time for a drink, Felix. It'll all be shut anyway.'

'Just do it. Park as close as you can to the front of the restaurant.'

Shaking my head, I do as he bids, and twenty seconds later we pull up outside the Dog.

'Don't turn the engine off, just let it tick over.'

'Felix, please tell me what the fuck we are doing here.'

'Follow me,' he says, and gets out of the car. He makes his way silently down the side alley between the Dog and the pub next door as I follow, trying not to step on anything in my bare feet. He goes through a small door at the rear of the restaurant, and I find myself inside a communal area with a staircase leading up. Felix starts up the stairs, and I grab him from behind.

'Where are we going?' I hiss.

'Just trust me. And try not to scream, you bloody girl.'

With a great sense of foreboding, I follow him up the stairs.

There's a door ajar at the top, and Felix enters, beckoning behind him for me to follow.

As we enter the flat, all the breath suddenly leaves my lungs. Light-headed, I grab the door-jamb to keep my balance as I stare at the body on the floor.

It's clearly Derek, and he's clearly very, very dead.

37

FELIX

I've always had a soft spot for Shakespeare. English was one of the subjects at school that I didn't just coast through waiting for the next break, but one in which I actually made an effort. It was his flair for the melodramatic, his poetic championing of injustice, and his passionate conviction that success was never beyond the everyman, provided he was willing to put in a little work, that attracted me to works like *Hamlet* and *Twelfth Night*.

Tonight though, it is the words of another far less appreciated wordsmith that spring to mind. It might sound like the Bard himself penned the immortal words, 'Oh what a tangled web we weave when first we practice to deceive,' but it was in fact the Scottish historian Sir Walter Scott. This prophetic aphorism implies that when you act deceitfully you set in motion a domino structure of complications that will inevitably spiral out of control. Old Sir Wally knew a thing or two about finding himself in a scrape. He suffered from polio, financial ruin and critical derision, held little respect for his fans and was in no small part responsible for the American Civil War. Yet there are busts of him all over Scotland.

He was a man who saw an opportunity and took it.

Adrenaline junkies throw themselves off high buildings; city traders toy with stocks and shares for profit; politicians manipulate people. We each have our own little ways of getting our kicks. But as perceptive as Scotty's tangled web idiom was, it implies that the deceitful chain of events invariably led to the downfall of the initiator, and that is where he and I disagree. Indeed, had he spent some time with yours truly, I firmly believe he would have changed his most famous saying to 'Oh what we can achieve when we deceive.'

I knew that Nevin was so strung out he was bound to sleep well tonight, especially after I crushed up two Zopiclone tablets and dissolved them in his third whisky. He was already listing to the side as he went in to brush his teeth and by half past ten I could hear him snoring loudly upstairs.

He had of course continued with his cross-examination of me when we got home from supper, worry lines etched all over his face as he considered the day ahead tomorrow. It had got to the point where I knew I had to do something about Derek, and for a brief while I considered bringing Nevin in on the act. That plan was kiboshed when I admitted that Nevin really does not cope well under pressure. A little sedative and a few hours of uninterrupted sleep were what he needed, and I could crack on with my infernal machinations without having to worry about him crashing the plane into the mountain.

While he was getting the kids ready for bed I had snuck into his room and gone through his drawers to find the blackest pieces of clothing he owned. Although he's a bit taller and significantly broader than me, I was looking for the black cycling jersey he frequently wore on our mini biking expeditions around various European towns. These had become less frequent over the past year as Gloria's agency business gained traction and Nevin was required to be at home more with the kids. I eventually found it tucked away at the back of his T-shirt drawer, and a pair of dark socks and the black trousers of his tuxedo set, which I found hanging in the dresser packed with Gloria's evening wear, completed my ensemble. As a last thought, I also grabbed a tube of Gloria's lip balm.

The evening air was balmy and dry as I made my way down the garden towards the coastal path leading into the town. It was only about a five-minute walk to the esplanade and I glanced at my Rolex, liberated from a minor royal's collection on a shooting weekend near Balmoral.

Ten to eleven. Perfect.

The seafront was relatively quiet, but I needed to be careful as it was nearly closing time for the pubs and restaurants that line the esplanade. I needed to be seen by as few people as possible. Even though I was dressed fully in black and without shoes on, the street lights cast an orange glow along the stretch and I was aware that I was fully visible. There were a few other late-night walkers ambling along with their dogs or arm in arm, lovers enjoying the romantic sea setting here in rural Devon.

The Old Sea Dog looked quiet from the outside, although I was sure there were still a few stragglers within, finishing their coffees after their evening meals or propped up at the bar having one last nightcap before closing. It didn't matter. I wasn't planning on going inside.

I strolled as casually as I could right past the open windows and doors of the restaurant, keeping my head down so I would not be visible to anyone looking out who might be able to furnish a description of my face at a later date. As soon as I was past it, I made a quick right turn into the small alleyway between the Dog and the pub next door. There were no lights down here except the rear security light from the kitchen restaurant, which I presumed was left on all night. It was dark enough though, and with my all-black gear I was confident no one had seen me.

The communal door was unlocked as before and I quietly slid it open, noting with no small relief how little noise my bare feet made. The inside corridor was completely dark, and I inched my way up the stairs towards the flat, praying a motion-sensing light wouldn't flick on. It didn't. That just left Derek's naughty little security camera in the hallway, which I negotiated by smearing Gloria's lip balm on the lens. The display screen must have been in the restaurant for him to watch my meeting with Gloria, so there was no way he could see me approaching from inside the flat itself.

I checked my watch. One minute to eleven. Taking a deep breath, I knocked very lightly on the door to the flat and heard footsteps approaching from inside.

'You're bang on time, sweetheart,' said a lascivious voice from the other side of the door. 'Boy oh boy, have I been looking forward to th–'

Derek stopped dead as he opened the door, expecting to see Gloria on the other side, but instead coming face to face with the very man whom he had earlier blackmailed.

'What the–'

Those were his final words as my fist shot out and jabbed a hard and fast blow right under his chin, crushing his windpipe and making him stagger back into the flat, his hands reaching for his throat. He choked, gasping for breath as he went down to his knees on the carpet, sheer bewilderment all over his pudgy chevy chase.

Calmly I stepped in and closed the door behind me. Derek's eyes began to boggle as he desperately tried to pull air into his lungs. I knew it would be easy to overpower him. Although we're roughly the same height he's probably got forty pounds on me in terms of weight, but he could have had a hundred and it wouldn't have mattered. It doesn't matter how big a bloke is: one swift blow to the larynx and anyone will go down.

I pulled a length of fishing rope out from where I had stuffed it behind my trousers and slowly walked behind Derek. On his knees he tried to turn his head around to see me, but the added pressure on his windpipe made him choke and splutter even more. I uncoiled the rope and wrapped it very quickly around his neck twice, then when I was sure the fraying fronds had secured, I jerked it up swiftly. He was too heavy to lift physically off the ground, but his own weight worked against him as the rope bit into his neck and he struggled even more in panic. His hands came away from his constricted larynx and he tried to work his fingers underneath the rope, desperately trying to ease the tension.

But the more he struggled the more the rope bit.

I wrapped the other end round my wrists a couple of times to secure it further and yanked upwards. I couldn't see Derek's face at that moment as I was behind him, but I knew his tongue would be forcing its way out of his mouth and his eyes would be getting more and more bloodshot as the pressure built.

I lifted the rope as high as I could and counted as slowly as my pounding heart would let me to thirty. His struggles stopped when I got to about fifteen but I kept the pressure on, hoisting as high as I could, my arm muscles burning with the effort.

Finally I released the rope and he immediately collapsed to the floor with a heavy thump. I hoped those still drinking in the restaurant underneath weren't too disturbed by the noise and vibration.

I removed the rope from around his neck and checked for a pulse. Nothing. I tucked the rope back into my trousers, left the door on the latch and made my way down the stairs, checking to see no one was coming out of the restaurant's kitchen into the communal area.

The whole thing took around forty-five seconds.

Derek wouldn't be giving us any trouble tomorrow after all.

38

NEVIN

'Oh Jesus Christ, Felix, what have you done?' I say as I stare at the portly body on the floor.

'What had to be done,' he says with finality. 'Now get his feet and help me lift him.'

I feel sick. A wave of nausea is coursing through my whole body, and I am struggling to hold on to consciousness. Felix seems to notice this, dropping Derek's shoulders and approaching me with determination in his eyes.

'When we get through with what we're about to do, I'm going to tell you a few home truths, Nevin. You may not like what you hear, but I'm telling you, there was no other choice and what I did was in our best interests and those of your children. Believe me, there was no alternative. Now I need you to focus, okay? *Nevin...*'

My breath is coming in short, ragged little gasps, and I suddenly feel a sharp sting on my cheek. Felix has slapped me around the face. Gently, and without any real pain, but it snaps me out of my fugue state and does a good job of bringing me back to reality.

Felix points to Derek's feet.

'Grab his legs and let's get him out to the car now.'

Panic is returning, but I don't fancy a stronger blow to the jaw this time so I'm forced to do as Felix says. I bend down and scoop my hands under Derek's sizeable ankles and hoist them upwards.

'Jesus, this fat bastard weighs a ton.' Felix grunts, as he struggles with the heavier end. 'We'll have to slide him down the stairs, okay?'

With supreme effort we scooch Derek's body along the rough pile of the carpet towards the door and manoeuvre him to the top of the stairs.

'Right, stop.' Felix pants, then with another huge effort lifts Derek into a sitting position. 'Now just to warn you, this might look and sound fairly brutal, so prepare yourself,' he says, before using his knees to shunt the body. Gravity takes over and Derek lolls head first down the stairs, toppling over and over himself until he comes to rest at the bottom in a crumpled heap, his head jammed into his own groin.

'Now comes the hard part,' Felix says, brushing past me and taking the stairs two at a time until he gets to the bottom. 'Come on. Morning is about to be broken.'

It takes us a good five minutes, but it seems like double that, to manipulate Derek along the alleyway. Felix stops just before it breaks into the esplanade and peers out to ensure the coast is clear.

'What about security cameras?' I whisper. I'm very worried that some, if not all, of the million-pound hotels along the seafront will be equipped with CCTV cameras that are bound to have picked us up

'Already checked. There are none until The Regency further along. As long as we go back the way we came we'll be in the clear.'

Having assured himself there are no early morning dog

walkers on the seafront he jogs swiftly out to the car and opens the boot, leaving me propping up Derek's head. It seems too callous to leave him lying on the concrete pavement. Felix runs back and grabs his shoulders and with much huffing and puffing we lift him over to the car. There is a moment of sheer panic as we realise Derek is too large to fit in the trunk. Felix thinks quickly and whispers, 'We'll have to put him across the back seats.'

He opens both rear doors and we hoist Derek's torso up and try to push him across the rear seats of the car. It doesn't work.

'Hold on,' says Felix, and he runs round to the other side, scooching himself across the seats so he can grab Derek's shirt before pulling him forcefully as I shunt him from the other side. The sun hasn't yet come over the horizon but we're both dripping with sweat as we finally manage to muscle the large body into the car, and with difficulty I bend his knees up so I can shut the door. He has already started to stiffen. I feel even more faint now than when I first saw his body, but Felix can't drive and has never even bothered to learn how, so it's up to me. I take a few deep breaths of the morning air to clear my head before jumping back into the driver's seat.

'Now remember, back the way we came,' says Felix as he straps himself in. 'Take it easy through the ford. We've got a lot more weight in the car this time around.'

The way he is speaking is so perfunctory, so matter of fact, that it belies the fact that we have a dead body sprawled across the rear seats.

'What happens if we get stopped?' I ask with alarm.

'It's four o'clock in the morning,' Felix hisses. 'Unless Treme has the world's friendliest milkman we'll be fine. We're only going a quarter of a mile. Now *drive*.'

With body-numbing trepidation I switch my concentration to driving the car home. Every turn I make, I am expecting to see a police car emerge behind us, and I am practically hyperventilating with relief when we pull up to Coastguard's Lane.

'Lights off, *ease* into the driveway,' Felix instructs.

He leaps out of the car once we come to a stop, snatches the car keys from me and heads to the garage door to unlock it. The morning is deathly still – the birds haven't started to cheep yet – and there is a surreal haze floating over the horizon.

Ten minutes later, just before the sun emerges and the birds begin their song, Derek's body splashes into the septic tank in the ground and cosies up next to my wife in a very different way to how he was planning a few hours earlier.

I only just make it back to my bed before collapsing on it and passing out through sheer nervous exhaustion.

39

NEVIN

I wake four hours later to the sound of conversation in the kitchen. Shuffling down the stairs I see Felix, back in his cycling gear, flipping pancakes at the stove with Amy and Josh chittering away while watching him.

'Morning Daddy,' Josh says.

'Ah, the Kraken awakes!' Felix intones cheerfully.

I wonder just how in the hell he can look so fresh after our middle-of-the-night excursion. He pours me a coffee and I sit down beside Amy, pulling her close to me for a hug. I ruffle Josh's crisp hair, which he gels to perfection like his hero Cristiano Ronaldo every morning.

'Kids, Uncle Fixly and I have a few things to sort out this morning, so how about I call Grandma Susie and you can go and play at hers for a few hours?'

Both kids groan simultaneously.

'She always makes us eat raw cabbage and onion,' Josh moans.

'It's called coleslaw, big guy,' Felix says laughing. 'And it's good for you!'

'It tastes like ass,' says Amy.

'Hey young lassie,' I say, affecting a stern Scottish brogue. 'If your mother heard you say that she'd kick ye oot of the hoose.'

'What she doesn't know can't hurt her,' Amy replies cleverly. 'And when is she coming home anyway?'

Oh God. At some point I'm going to have to tell them the truth. That Mummy is never coming home. *Well, she is home, but not in the way you think.* Another bout of unease suddenly arrests my stomach.

'Your mummy is having a few days off,' Felix says, flipping the frying pan. 'She'll be back before you know it. Now, who's for *maple syrup?*'

The kids both shout 'Me!' and I wonder how the hell I'm going to explain everything to them. Thankfully, just then Josh's ears prick up as he hears a vehicle approaching up the lane.

'Mummy's back!' he shouts and runs to the porch. 'Oh, it's just a lorry. Daddy, there's a lorry coming up the drive.'

Shit. The concrete's arrived!

'Uh, kids, stay here with Uncle Fixly, I'm just going to sort out The Man.'

To the kids, any adult who arrives to engage in a grown-up issue, and therefore one of supreme disinterest to them, is 'The Man'. The Man comes to trim the hedges. The Man sorts out Daddy's taxes. Whoever invented The Man is one of nature's greatest miracles.

I glance at Felix as I head out of the door and he winks at me, inferring that in about ten minutes all our problems will be solved. I have to say, once this unpleasant business is out of the way I will feel a great deal easier about the situation. I might even be able to have a few of Felix's pancakes.

There is yet another moment of terror when the concrete dude inserts the nozzle in the manhole of the septic tank as I think he's about to get down on all fours and take a look inside it to satisfy his curiosity.

'Can I get you a tea or coffee, mate?' I shout in the hope of distracting him.

'Tea please, guv, milk and four sugars.'

Four sugars?

'I think we're out of sugar, I'm afraid, I've got stevia if that's okay?'

'Better stick five in then.' He sniffs, and that seems to have done the trick as he makes his way back to the rear of the truck without examining the hole he's about to fill.

'How long will this take?' I ask, never taking my eyes off him in case he decides he needs another look.

He glances at his piece of paper, his job sheet. 'Between four and six cubic metres... not long. Ten, maybe fifteen minutes.'

I don't ask him how long it will take to cure as I don't want to engage him any more than necessary. But I read online that it can take up to forty-eight days until it's fully solid. I wait until the liquid concrete starts to pour before I head back to the porch and call in to Felix to fix a cup of milky tea with five spoonfuls of stevia. I shiver at the thought of it.

No sooner had the truck pulls out of the driveway than Lorraine, my curious neighbour, appears at the end of the drive looking flushed. She is waving this morning's edition of *The Treme Chronicle*.

'Oh my goodness, Nevin, I've just seen the paper. We had no idea! What has happened? Is there anything we can do?'

I'm mildly touched by her concern, but I just know that she is loving this unexpected hit of drama in her otherwise pedestrian day.

'Yes, it's been a hard couple of days,' I say, easily looking downcast. 'I'm afraid there isn't much I can tell you, Lorraine. Do you mind if I take a look at that?'

I reach for her paper and another wave of fear rushes over

me as I see Gloria's picture on the front page. It's the photo I gave the police. The one of her smiling and wrapped in a thick throw from when we had an impromptu beach barbecue two weeks ago.

'Of *course*. Oh, it's just terrible! I haven't even had a chance to read the article yet. I was so worried I came right over to see you.'

I scan the text.

> Worry as local woman is reported missing
>
> Police are appealing for information after a Treme woman was reported missing from the area yesterday.
>
> Gloria Campbell, 35, of Cliff Road, was last seen on Thursday night whilst celebrating with friends and family at her husband Nevin's fortieth birthday party.
>
> Police say they are concerned she may have gone for a late-night swim and got into trouble. The coastguard has been alerted and a search is under way of the coastline from Axmouth to Budleigh Salterton.
>
> Mrs Campbell, a literary agent, moved to the area less than a month ago from Somerset. She is an active member of the local community and her two young children attend St Peter's School. Her husband Nevin is an author whose novels regularly top the political thriller genre of Amazon's bestseller lists…

I can't read any more as Lorraine is buzzing my ear, so I hand her back the paper and try to calm her down.

'Lorraine, I'm afraid now isn't really the best time to talk. I have to go down to the police station and see if any information has come in.'

'Of course, of *course*, darling,' she says, sounding very sympathetic. 'Absolutely. If there is anything Chris and I can do, you must let us know, please. We did wonder when we saw the police car, but we had no idea it was for something as dreadful as this. How are the children coping?'

'Well, to be honest, I haven't really broken it to them just yet. I'm hoping this is all going to be resolved before I need to.'

I indicate that's the end of the conversation by turning and walking back towards the cottage and she rather reluctantly heads back towards her own property. No sooner than she has left do I get a call on my mobile, and another wave of anxiety washes over me as I realise it's the police station's number.

'Mr Campbell? Sergeant Kelliher again. I'm sure you will be aware by now that your wife's disappearance has made the papers. Not something we could avoid, I'm afraid. However, it may help us if there are any sightings from members of the public.'

'What about CCTV? Is there anything that shows that area of the beach?' I ask with a definite ulterior motive.

'I'm afraid not, Mr Campbell. There are no public CCTV cameras on the esplanade, much to our continued frustration. The district council continues to fob us off with budget concerns.'

I breathe a sigh of relief, but my hubris wants to continue pressing the point. 'Come on, the whole country is covered by a camera somewhere. There must be *some* footage you can look at?'

'The vast majority of CCTV cameras are not operated by government bodies, but by private individuals or companies, usually to monitor the interiors of shops and businesses. We have already been along that stretch to ask local firms if they have any, but apart from one camera that covers the front of The Regency Hotel, I'm afraid there is nothing to speak of. We've had a look at that footage and haven't been able to determine anything on the evening in question. I know it's not what you want to hear right now, but I assure you we are doing everything within our power to ensure your wife is found.'

Do I detect a note of accusation in his voice?

'Please can I ask you to remain at home for now, at least until we hear from the coastguard,' he goes on. 'I understand they are preparing a helicopter as we speak.'

Bloody hell. I cringe at the thought of the unnecessary expense this is going to cost the coastguard and the police force, but what choice do I have? I can hardly tell them to suspend the search as she is buried in a well of concrete in my garage.

'I understand. Well, keep me informed,' I say with as much gravitas as I can muster.

'We'll be sending a family liaison officer to you later today to help.'

'Uh, that won't be necessary at this time,' I say with uncertainty. 'I haven't actually informed the children their mother is missing at this stage, just in case something turns up today.'

'If you're sure, Mr Campbell. However I do advise that you let the children know sooner rather than later, especially as they are bound to come into contact with school friends and colleagues on Monday if not before. The liaison officer will assist you with that process...'

'Thank you, I will take that under advisement. If I need anything I will let you know.'

'Very well, I'll call you later with any update,' he says, and hangs up.

I stare at my phone screen, lost in thought. I'm sure I detected a note of accusation in his voice. But then don't all police sound like that, trained to be suspicious of everyone? I get the sinking feeling that he's just leading me on until the cops can amass enough evidence to arrest me. And Felix as well. At least the official angle seems to be the 'late-night swim that went wrong', rather than any suspicions of foul play at having found my blood all over her dress.

With any luck, the search will peter out after a couple of days and everyone will go about assuming she's been lost at sea and how terrible it must be for her poor husband and kids. An incredible weight lifts from me as I realise I may not have to do some sort of garbled press conference appealing for her return. That would have been the ultimate test of my cool and calm exterior, and I'm not sure I could have coped.

I head back inside the house for a plate of pancakes, suddenly feeling like I might just get away with this after all.

40

FELIX

Doing away with Derek is starting to look more and more like a masterstroke on my part. Nevin hasn't clocked it yet, but I have no doubt that the filth will be knocking on his door once they discover that not only has his wife gone missing but the owner of a local restaurant as well. They are bound to put two and two together and the theory will arise that Gloria and Derek have run off together, as absurd as that may seem, especially when they question local residents and ascertain they were close friends. And that's a theory I shall do my utmost to reinforce to them. I'm just waiting for Nevin to click so I can lead him down this path, but understandably his mind has been focused on other things this morning, like that damnably nosy neighbour and the phone call he just received which was clearly from the cops.

As he comes back in I set a large plate of pancakes, maple syrup and berries on the table and indicate for him to get stuck in.

But it seems he has something else on his mind. 'Kids,' he says, looking like he's about to break some dreadful news. 'There's something I have to tell you. It's about Mummy.'

Shit. I knew this was coming, but I had hoped to get him on his own first so I could steer him through the process. Looks like he'll have to handle this one on his own, so I sit down at the table with them all and look appropriately serious.

'What about Mummy?' Amy says, looking concerned.

'The thing is,' Nevin says, clearly grasping for the best way to go about this. 'Mummy hasn't gone away for a few days. I mean, she has, but... Look, I'm just going to say it. You may be hearing from some people that Mummy has disap... that she has gone missing.'

Both of the kids are staring enrapt at their father. Amy swallows and Josh stops chewing.

'Who is saying that?' Amy asks in a very little voice.

'The police are, sweetheart. The thing is, when Mummy went away a couple of days ago, she didn't tell me, or anyone, where she was going. And now it looks as though she might have... got a bit lost.'

Jesus, Nevin. Is this the best you can do?

'But she'll be able to find her way back, won't she?' Josh says.

'I don't know if she will, darling,' says Nevin, reaching over and putting a supportive hand on his son's shoulder. 'You see, the thing with grown-ups is, sometimes they just decide they need to get away for a while. Life can be difficult for adults, which is something you will come to understand as you get older, but sometimes people go away and then... decide not to come back.'

Amy is scrutinising her father, confused and wondering what to say next. Nevin is about to speak again, but I kick him under the table and give him a look suggesting he let them process it and come back with any more questions before he digs himself further into this hole.

'Does Mummy not want to live with us anymore?' she finally says.

'It's not that, honeybunch,' Nevin says. 'Of course she does. Mummy would never choose to leave us all on purpose. What I'm saying is that when Mummy went away, something might have happened to her that means she is unable to come back.'

'Is she dead?' Josh asks, trying to hold back tears.

'We don't know that,' I say, thinking it's an appropriate time for me to cut in and give Nevin a bit of slack. 'We just don't know right now where she is. But the police are looking for her, and the most important thing is for us all to stay strong and pray that she returns home safe and sound, okay?'

'But, I don't understand,' Amy says quietly. 'Has someone taken her?'

'No, nobody has taken her,' says Nevin firmly. 'It's important that you understand that.'

'Then why doesn't she come back?' asks Josh, who is now openly weeping.

Nevin looks at his son, stumped. I decide it's time to level with the kids.

'The thing is, kids, your mother might have gone for a swim in the sea and then got lost and not been *able* to find her way back.'

There is silence around the table as the kids take this in.

'Then she could be dead,' Amy says with finality.

'As I say, we don't know that yet, sweetheart,' says Nevin. 'We just have to hope that someone finds her and helps her. She might have swum all the way to France by mistake and you know Mummy, she doesn't speak any French!'

I can see what Nevin is doing. He's trying to soften the blow. But kids are nothing if not full of hope, and leading them on with misinformation is only going to cause them more upset down the line.

'It's possible that your mother might not be coming back,' I say gently. And Nevin looks at me with horror. But I believe selective information is not the way to go here.

'What we're going to do is try and continue to go on with our lives as best we can for the time being,' he says. 'And maybe in a while we'll come to understand a little more about what happened. I'm sorry, kids, I'm so very sorry.'

Nevin can't hold it back any longer and breaks down in tears. Josh looks the most shocked. He has probably never seen his father cry before. That's a watershed moment for a young boy. The moment he sees that his father, his rock, the man who seems a hundred feet tall, is human and vulnerable just like everybody else.

Now would be a good time to give them some space, so I stand up, pat Josh and Amy gently on their heads as the tears flow, and head out into the garden. I stand and gaze at the ocean and the horizon in the heat of the mid-morning. I suppose I should feel more. I should feel remorse and guilt that my actions have led to so much pain.

But all I can think is, *get a load of that view.*

41

NEVIN

ONE WEEK LATER

I am a terrible person. I am a terrible father. And I am a liar. I've lied to my own kids. What on earth could have possessed me to think that any of this was a good idea? I wish I had a time machine so I could go back to a week ago, no, a *month* ago, and take the whole damn thing back. The affair, the divorce, even the effing birthday party. I'd just refuse point blank to have it and take my wife and kids on holiday somewhere for a month. Maybe even never come back.

The torture of hindsight.

Now my kids are irrevocably scarred, they have lost their mother and, worst of all, they think she's abandoned them. What the heck sort of battle armour is that to provide them with as they enter the most important and formative phase of their lives?

And I'm a widower.

I'm a widower who can't even act like one. I have to go through the rest of my life pretending to all and sundry I'm hopeful that one day my wife will show up again. When the searing truth is that I will never see her again. Nobody will. Well, at least until long into the future when they raze

Coastguard's Cottage to the ground or it drops into the sea. But that's not going to happen for maybe a couple of hundred years, and it will be a heck of a surprise to whatever future beachcomber comes across *that* pile of concrete. They might even look back through the records to find out who the previous owners were, and will discover that the woman who used to own it went missing two hundred years ago and was never found. The mystery will be solved. Maybe they'll have invented technology by then that will be able to bring me back from the dead to stand trial for it all.

I must be going mad. I'm worrying about being arrested in the year 2223. I should be worried about being arrested right now.

But the longer this goes on the more tentatively comfortable I'm becoming with it.

The police called off the search for Gloria three days ago. The sergeant was right. It did make the national news, and for four days straight we had news crews and reporters camping outside our house at the end of the lane. I couldn't even take the kids out the front without somebody snapping us with a long lens. Gloria's face was on the news every night and most of the day, and it was undoubtedly the biggest news story in the country for about seventy-two hours. It was of course compounded by the fact that Derek, the local restaurateur, had also disappeared. And that's when the conjecture started.

The rumours were that he and Gloria were having an affair and had run off together. Chat shows drafted in experts who speculated in droves how difficult it was to fake one's death and escape the country without detection. Alerts were put out across Europe by Interpol, broadcasting Gloria and Derek's picture and instructing border patrols to be on the look-out for a British couple with obviously fake passports. Everywhere I went I could feel eyes burning holes in the back of my head. I was the talk of the town. There were sympathisers, but there were also the more suspicious, those who gave me a wide berth and were no doubt peddling the rumours that I had discovered the affair and done away with Gloria and Derek. They can't prove it, of course.

Amazingly, sightings cropped up all over the south-west, and even in places like Scotland and Northern Ireland. People claimed to have seen a couple acting suspiciously who matched the descriptions that were circulating on the news. In Suffolk, police broke down the door of an Airbnb cottage after a tip-off, and a real couple, who, I shit you not, were actually engaged in an affair, were rumbled. But of course, they weren't Derek and Gloria. They were just shamed on the national news. I bet *they* regret it too.

Then, all of a sudden, the coverage stopped. The police announced that the search for Gloria and Derek, in this area anyway, was over. And just like that the news crews disappeared and we were left, shell-shocked, as they took off somewhere else to cover another more topical story. Today's news is tomorrow's fish and chips wrapper and all that. It really is true.

And Felix was true to his word of sticking by me until the smoke had dissipated. He's still here, fawning over the kids, helping me with the chores and still trying to charm Susan. Susan, who I'm convinced still thinks I am responsible somehow.

It made me think, how many people did actually get away with murder? How many crimes went unsolved because of sheer happenstance? You couldn't write it. Well, maybe I could. It certainly gave me some plot ideas for my next novel. But when I'll actually get back to writing again is anyone's guess. All I can focus on now is my children, making sure they are coping and not balancing an inch from the precipice like I am.

I think for a few days I was the most recognisable man in the country. I'm convinced Felix was even slightly jealous of me. I'm actually looking forward to my next royalty cheque as I've no doubt this little episode has fuelled sales of my books. My debut novel is even shooting back up the Amazon charts again.

But as Plautus said, 'Nothing is more wretched than the mind of a man conscious of guilt.' And different people cope with guilt in different ways. It is the strangest of emotions, one that festers in the mind and tugs at your heart until you give into it. Guilt functions as a means of guiding us in the right direction.

Maybe that's why I took the decision to write it all down. Last night while Felix and the kids were asleep and another long heavy night stretched out in front of me, I crept out to the garage, fired up my PC, and, sitting less than a metre away from my dead wife, I committed the whole damn thing to Microsoft Word. Maybe it's my way of coping with what I've done. I've always been able to rationalise better when I see things in print form. Plot lines, dream interpretations, inspirational sayings, even shopping lists. I'm sure if Felix knew he'd go absolutely apeshit. But if it helps me come to terms, even one per cent better with the whole sordid experience, then I will consider it a successful undertaking. How long I'll have to wait to feel its benefit I don't know, or even if I ever will. Perhaps I'm hoping that one day, when I'm a lot greyer and a lot older, I'll be able to read it back and reflect that it maybe wasn't the worst thing that ever happened to me. My life would have to take a pretty drastic turn for the worse if that is to be the case.

But right now, that one per cent is all I'm holding onto.

42

FELIX

When you stay in one place for an extended amount of time one of two things can happen. One, you get itchy feet and feel the urge to move on to greener pastures, as soon as. Two, the longer you stay the more you become immured to the place, as if an invisible force is holding you there almost against your will. You become used to the foibles and practices of daily life, and if you're not careful it can become a little too comfortable.

It depends what kind of person you are. I've always been what people might call a free spirit, although more through necessity than nature. A bit like the alien species in *Independence Day,* who arrive at a planet, consume all the natural resources and obliterate the indigenous population, then hop in their hyperdrive and move on to the next civilisation. It's not the most literate of comparisons, but that's just the way I've always done things. Once I've extracted all I can from a place or person it's time to move on and find a new source. It's not purely selfish – I'm also thinking of the host. Having someone hang around like a bad smell can get very irritating, especially if that someone is looking to extend the good-time vibes they brought with them beyond their host's natural tolerance.

Get in, get done, get gone. That's always been my motto.

But the problem with this sort of transient, almost parasitic existence is that once you find a steady supply of satisfaction the thought of moving on becomes a burden. Like a flea in a blood bank, you have no need to seek alternative sustenance.

And I think that's what is happening to me in Treme-on-Sea. After two decades of spreading myself thin leaping from host to host I've come to realise that this place may well be *my* blood bank.

When my father kicked me out at the age of eighteen, I was almost grateful. A weight was lifted. The weight of *expectance*. It instilled in me the importance of fending for myself, and how asinine it was to be beholden to a false sense of paternity just because it was what was expected. It didn't make me feel unwanted, it just made me hungrier to prove that I didn't need his help or his money. It didn't inspire in me a dedicated work ethic or ambition to achieve, it just made me realise that if I wanted anything out of life then I had to find others to provide it for me. You may call that entitlement, and I suppose you'd be right. I didn't care. I got what I wanted by hook or by crook. Actually no, not by crook, by the sheer force of my own character. I used what I had been gifted, my looks and my charisma. I'm no different to an actor in that sense. Do you begrudge Tom Cruise his millions? No, because he uses what he was born with to its best effect.

But like any drug, the high is the best part. It's easy to continue that high if you keep using, but most normal people aren't blessed with never-ending tolerance and at some point you have to either stop, or die. The drug of Felix provides a very pure high, but there comes a point where no matter how much you take, it never has the same effect as that first hit.

And I fear that Nevin has just about hit that point with me. Despite everything I've done for him over the past week he's coming down from the euphoria and is realising that either he continues fixing or something will have to crack. It's the classic tell of someone trying to get rid of a guest who is overstaying their welcome at the end of the party. The stretching, the heavy yawn, the exclamation that wow, that was one hell of a night, but now I think it's time I hit the hay. I can read him so well.

It's a shame, not least for me because I'm not ready to move on yet. I'm ready to set down my roots and let them burrow into the sandy beaches of Devon, more specifically Treme. It's just how I go about persuading Nevin that that state of affairs is in his best interests too. That is the challenge now...

43

NEVIN

After the chaos of the last week I'm looking forward to getting back a sense of normalcy in mine and the kids' lives. Albeit without their mother.

Kids need routine. Routines help them feel safe and build healthy habits. They also help parents feel organised, reduce stress and find time for enjoyable activities.

There, self-help book consulted.

The first thing I do is print off a weekly planner, and I intend to sit down with them and run through their school timetable. Josh's evening football training, Amy's piano practice and drama workshops, planned weekends away visiting friends and relatives, things like that. I need to get back into my daily schedule of writing when they're at school. It's time to step up and be a responsible single dad. I should also get round to writing some kind of will, which is something Gloria and I always put off for another day. I realise that because Gloria has died intestate her estate passes directly to me, as her husband. What there is of it anyway. Her estate consists of her business and the house. All the savings are in my name, simply because I've been the major earner over the last thirteen years and all my royalties automatically go into my account. We have a joint account, which I put money into for daily household needs like food shopping and petrol. But all the bills, the utilities, council tax, insurance and others are automatically debited from my account each month. Gloria also has her own account, but I can't imagine there's very much in it. Still, that's something that probate will deal with.

I'm not naïve enough to think this will be an easy ride, but by following a routine I'm hoping that it won't be too long before we get back in our stride and the recent events will soon seem like a distant memory. Kids are very adaptable as you know.

There's just one small fly in the ointment. Felix. He doesn't seem to be showing any desire or intention to move on. Don't get me wrong, I'm indebted to him for sticking by me through thick and thin, not just in the last week but for many years. He has been the kind of emotional support I didn't even realise I needed. But for my own sanity, and the stability that Amy and Josh need now, I kind of need him to be on his way. The longer he sticks around, the more used they are getting to him being here, and I know it will be a tearful goodbye. But all honeymoons must come to an end, for want of a more appropriate analogy, and it's time for him to return to the much more sporadic presence in our lives that he has always been.

He insisted on being here for at least a few more days when the kids went back to school on Monday in order to help us adapt to the new schedule. At first I was grateful, but by Wednesday afternoon we'd done very little but potter around the house and garden, him reassuring me that everything was watertight, and I still hadn't written a single word of my new novel.

Now it's Thursday morning and he's in the shower again seemingly preparing for another day of breeze-shooting with absolutely zero intention of going anywhere. He must have washed his cycling clothes four or five times, borrowing clothes from my wardrobe while they dried in the sun, before climbing back into them. And there went another day.

Maybe I shouldn't be so hard on him. No doubt he has been affected by everything as well. He's not had any time to focus on his social calendar and work out where his next jolly might be. Maybe I'll leave it for a few more days. Procrastination can be a fine tool, and these things usually sort themselves out anyway. I'm sure once he gets itchy feet he'll be out the door quicker than a greyhound with a stick of dynamite up its arse.

He strolls into the kitchen with a wet towel wrapped around his lithe and muscular frame. It must take a heck of a lot of exercise to maintain that physique. I admit I'm slightly jealous. I'm definitely in worse shape than I should be for a man of my age, especially now that I'm in my forties. *Jesus, how did that happen so fast?* It only seems like yesterday we were celebrating my thirtieth in Portugal. That was a hell of a week too.

'So, matey boy, what's on the agenda for today?' he says merrily. 'I thought we might take a cycle over to that farm shop on the A37 before we collect the kids from school? I've heard spectacular things about their organic fruit aisle. All locally produced, you know. Or how about that garden centre on the way out of town? Your chrysanthemums are looking a bit thin. I think they could do with some blood and bone.'

Is this the same Felix who last month was partying on a yacht in the Caribbean with several members of the Argentinian national polo team? Something of a dichotomy.

'I wouldn't want to bore you with all that, mate,' I say self-deprecatingly. 'Didn't you say you had some big poker game in Italy coming up?'

'Oh that? Nah, I'm giving that a miss this year,' he replies off-handedly. 'Did you know Ryanair are stopping flights to

Naples? Bloody travesty if you ask me. I'm not cycling all that way.'

'Thought you usually fly first class?'

'Only when I'm not paying for it.'

'You could always take the Eurostar? If funds are a bit low, mate, I can always spot you the cash.'

'Don't get me started on European trains, old herring. They might sound romantic, but they're like national jigsaw puzzles. An ineffective patchwork of bollocks. Cross-border politics? We get enough of that here with Brexit. Do you know I had to queue for an hour and a half at Bristol just to get through customs?'

'Yeah, but we have blue passports now,' I joke.

'Europe is a shambles, mate. It's enough to make me want to hang up my skis full time.'

'What, no more jollies to Lars Braunholtz's winter palace?'

'I'll let you in on a little secret, my old lamb chop. Lars is swimming in debt and his winter palace is a two-bedroom chalet in Borovets. I nearly lost a toe to frostbite last time I was there. Appearances can be deceiving. No one knows that better than me...'

'Really? So what's your next move then?' I ask tentatively.

'I don't know,' he sighs, 'you know, I quite like it around here. I'm seriously thinking of finding myself a little pied-à-terre by the sea, like your good self.'

'Are you serious?' I ask, astonished by the image of Felix staying in one place for more than two weeks.

'Why not? I've got to do it sometime. I've grown tired of the nomadic life,' he says with a rococo sweep of his arms. 'It's all so... diluted.'

I suddenly feel an overwhelming urge to put him off this plan. 'Devon isn't all it's cracked up to be, mate. For a start it's actually only sunny for about three weeks of the year. You'd lose your tan.'

'Tan-schman. That's what salons are for.'

'You're serious, aren't you?'

'As a collapsed lung, my old cream tea.'

He vigorously dries his hair and goes over to the kettle to put on another pot of coffee. 'What do you reckon I could get around here for a grand a month?'

'I don't mean to be uncouth, mate, but not much.'

'I don't need much. A couple of bedrooms, a small garden, maybe a sea view?'

'You could try Brenham, it's a bit estate-y but you get more for your buck than anywhere around here.'

'I like it around here though. It's got a quaint sort of vibe. Plus, I'd be nearer you to help out with the kids and all that.'

'Felix, I don't mean to sound ungrateful, but the kids and I are going to be fine. They're not quite the handful they were when they were toddlers. They're more grown up now. In a year or so I'll actually be able to leave them on their own for a while if I need to.'

'Mate, come on,' he gushes. 'You think teenagers are easy? You'll have your hands full when Amy starts bringing home boys and Josh... well, when Josh sets his sights on something other than football.'

'Susan's only down the road. She's going to have a lot more time on her hands when she retires next year.'

'Susan?! She's hardly a fitting role model. Unless you want Amy to think she can pout her way through life...'

'Oh, and you are a fitting role model?' I interrupt.

He turns on me with a dangerous look in his eyes.

I realise I've completely overstepped the mark. 'Felix, I'm sorry, mate, I didn't mean that to come out the way it did.'

He stares at me for a split second longer than is comfortable, and I get the impression that last comment has really eaten into him. When he speaks, it's with a tone of sincerity and sombreness that I rarely hear him use.

'That's a tad salty, don't you think? Considering all I've done for you in the past two weeks?'

'Felix, I'm incredibly grateful, you know that.'

'You know things would be a lot different around here if it wasn't for yours truly,' he says touchily. 'Just remember that, Nevin.'

He slowly walks out of the kitchen and I hear him padding up the stairs to get dressed. Oh dear, I might actually have pissed him off. There's a time for harsh truths, and there's a time to be a little more tactful. I should have chosen the latter. It's unlike Felix to do anything other than deflect when it comes to serious conversation.

I get the impression he feels I owe him a great deal more than I realise.

44

NEVIN

I can tell Felix is still smarting from my earlier implication that he is not the best role model for my children. I don't think I'm imagining it, but he was definitely a little testy with me all day.

To placate him I went along with his idea to cycle to the farm shop along the road out of town. It was a fairly easy three-mile ride there, and sure enough, as soon as he got his nose into a pile of artisanal cheese he perked up. He'd listened intently as the producer intoned in detail how she used smoked applewood to bring out its flavour, muttering 'marvellous' and 'fascinating' as she described the process. It's almost as if he's trying extra hard to blend in. As if embracing a provincial attitude will ingratiate him with the locals. When all it actually does is make him look like a condescending towny who's sussing out second home destinations. It's very unlike Felix, and I think he might be dead serious about setting down roots in Devon. And more specifically Treme-on-Sea.

The kids have finally gone to sleep and we're sitting on the wooden deck at the back of the cottage, sipping whisky as the last of the sun disappears below the line where the ocean meets the sky. I decide it's time to once again raise the subject to see how genuine he is, and maybe steer him back to the idea of rekindling a life of roving and debauchery, if only so I can live it vicariously through him.

'You know if you want, we can ask around a few estate agencies tomorrow and see what might be up for rent in the area,' I suggest, silently hoping he will brush off the idea and tell me he is in fact heading to St Tropez first thing. But he looks at me with what I can only describe as an expression of sheer relief.

'I thought you were against the idea of me moving here?' he says.

How does he do that? Turn a leading question right back around on me with just a few words?

'I never said that. I just happen to know what you're like, Felix. You're hardly the type of guy who chairs parish council meetings and organises charity whist drives. You'll spend one month here and go mad with boredom.'

'You really don't know me at all, do you?' he marvels. 'I mean, all these years and you still don't understand.'

'Understand what? Help me out here.'

'I would have thought you'd be the first to understand what it's like to be trapped.'

'Felix, I'm sorry. You mean to say you're dissatisfied with the life you have? I find it hard to believe that a man who never spends more than three nights at the same hotel feels trapped.'

'Why?' he says, a little too loudly. 'Why is that so hard to believe, Nevin? You think I want to spend the rest of my days living like a... a *diamond hobo*? Never having anywhere I can actually call *home*? You don't think that I've hankered after somewhere like that every day for the last twenty years?'

I'm slightly taken aback by this outburst, and also with the phrase 'diamond hobo', which I think is pure genius and one I must remember when I start writing again. *What a book title. And this year's Booker prize goes to.... Nevin Campbell for The Diamond Hobo!*

'I know what everyone thinks,' he goes on. 'Old Felix Van Arnhem, that leathery socialite who could charm the pants off a nun in Lourdes. Whose nickname is 'Crime' because he doesn't pay. The only man in history to insure his own cock! You think it's easy making friends when every single person I'm introduced to is wondering how much I'm going to fleece them for?'

I'm looking down at my knees because I know I'm guilty of perpetuating at least two of those rumours. Also because I'm rendered speechless in the face of this honest outpouring of emotion from Felix.

'I know I haven't lived the most austere life. And yes, I may have chosen to project this aura of an irresistible playboy, but it wasn't like I had any other options. It's fine for you, Nevin, you've actually got a talent for something other than cutting holes in rich people's pockets and waiting for the spare change to tumble out by their feet.'

'Felix, I had no idea you felt this way,' I say. I'm very ashamed I haven't noticed that my best friend has actually been living a lie for so long. 'I just assumed you loved it all; the parties, the mistresses, the free holidays...'

'I know what you are thinking, woe is Felix! I know I don't deserve sympathy. I've conned, womanised and gambled my way through my entire adult life, but do you not think that there is even a small part of me that needs to be more than just a beautiful façade, an advert for elitism, a poster boy for a life of excess who has absolutely fuck-all to call his own? That's what makes this whole thing so absurd, Nevin. The truth is, I'd have given anything for what you had two weeks ago. A sense of security, of belonging somewhere. And now I've gone and screwed all that up as well. For me, for you, for Josh and Amy, and most of all, for Gloria.'

He takes another sip of his whisky and stares at the ocean in front of him. Suddenly it makes sense to me. What all of this was actually for.

'Is that what all this is about, Felix?' I ask him, anger and disbelief clouding my voice. 'Was all this just so you could have what I have? So you could have *Gloria?*'

He looks at me with burning eyes. 'You arrogant, conceited son of a bitch. Do you honestly not get it?'

'Get what?! That you coveted my wife? My home? That you secretly just wanted it all for yourself?'

His face softens and he stands slowly. He sets down his whisky on the railing of the deck and takes a few paces in my direction. A stab of fear runs through me and I wonder if he's about to attack me, punch me, or worse, just walk away and never come back again leaving me with my last furious outburst echoing in my ears. He kneels down and puts his hands on my knees, then brings his eyes up to mine as if staring deep into my soul.

'I didn't want Gloria for myself, Nevin. Nothing could be further from the truth.'

He leans closer, so his face is just inches from mine, and I've never been so scared in my whole life.

'I wanted you, Nevin. It's always been you.'

The fear in my chest is replaced by utter disbelief before Felix tilts his head and brings his lips to mine.

45

FELIX

'Jesus Christ, Felix! What the hell are you doing?' Nevin shouts as he pulls away from me. 'Is this some sort of sick game?'

Okay, *not* the reaction I was hoping for. Perhaps he's just in shock. Wait a minute, then try a different approach.

'Okay, just keep your voice down. You'll wake the kids,' I say gently, trying to sound like a reasonable man, if not a reasonable fool.

'You've got to be joking,' Nevin says incredulously. 'I don't even know where to start... *this* was your plan all along? To get rid of my wife so you could have *me*?'

Now the cat's out of the bag. I suppose I'll have to come clean.

I've always been in love with Nevin. It started as a confused crush the first week we met at university. Back then I didn't really know who I was or what I felt. You have to remember, this was the late nineties when homophobia was still considered acceptable, often even encouraged. Even now I don't think of myself as gay. And it certainly wouldn't have allowed me to pursue the kind of lifestyle I have if I'd come out back then. I also knew that if I did ever want to reconcile with my father, the one thing that would make that impossible was if he knew the truth about my feelings for another man. And in my naïveté I still thought it was possible that he would welcome me back if I made a success of myself, regardless of who I chose to be with. So I continued to live my real life in secret, with the conquests and affairs splashed over the society pages masking my real desires.

But here's the thing, I've never fallen in love with anyone, male, female or otherwise.

Only Nevin.

And part of me knew that deep down he felt the same. All I have to do is make him see it for himself.

'Nevin, please don't fly off the handle,' I say, holding my hands out. 'Just let me explain and you'll understand.'

'Is this another one of your attempts to manipulate me so you can get what you want? Another play from the Van Arnhem book of *How To Con Your Way Through Life?* Because let me tell you, Felix, it may work with lust-blind heiresses and bi-curious playboys, but I'm your *best friend!*'

'This is not what you think it is,' I say, stepping towards him. Nevin backs further away from me with every inch I move. 'It was never my intention to deceive you or lure you into anything. I swear, Nevin. I know I've done some questionable things in my life; I know I've cajoled myself into many a pocket and even more beds over the years, but none of it made me any *happier*. Only the thought of one day being able to stand in front of you and tell you how I felt was what drove me on. This is not some game! This is my confession to you. *You* are what I really wanted.'

Nevin stares at me, bewildered. He takes a further step back before realising he's up against the rail of the decking and can't go any further. 'I can't believe this,' he says quietly. 'Everything you've done, all of it, has been because you're living a lie? For Christ's sake, Felix, you *murdered* a man!'

'I did it for you, Nevin. No, I did it for *us!* So we could stop pretending...'

'The only one who's pretending is you, Felix. You've been pretending your whole life.'

'Don't you think I know that? Do you not comprehend that it's for that precise reason that the dam broke? My whole life has been a tissue of lies, an orgy of deception, and I can't do it anymore! You must realise yourself, there's only so high you can build a skyscraper before nature takes over and it comes crumbling to the ground! When you approached me all those weeks ago about getting rid of Gloria, it was like a crushing weight had been lifted off me. Don't you see? I knew then that you had finally realised that *you* were living a lie too. That this... *mask* we've been living behind for twenty years could finally be torn off! You've been faking it too, Nevin. Don't try and deny it. You've just done it in a way society deems acceptable. The unhappy marriage, the cottage by the sea, the two perfect children... it's all a veneer disguising the man you were meant to be!'

'And just who *am* I supposed to be, Felix?'

'You're supposed to be with me! There's no point in denying it anymore. You think everything that has happened was just luck dealing us a great hand? It was *fate,* Nevin, it was meant to be! And now we no longer have to be afraid, we no longer have to *pretend.* Fate has finally delivered into our hands everything that we need. Us! You and me together!'

Suddenly Nevin bolts off the deck and runs into the garden. I'm so shocked my feet remain bolted to the floor, before I snap out of it and leap down the steps after him.

'You can't run from it any longer, Nevin!' I shout, no longer caring if the neighbours hear us. 'Stop, please, let's talk about this. It's our time now!'

He reaches the end of the garden and disappears through the gap in the hedge, into the scrubland beyond. When I finally catch him up he's standing by the summer house, leaning on it to catch his breath. I'm running so fast I have to put the brakes on to stop myself careening into him. He turns to me, his brown eyes seeming to blaze with the last of the fire reflected from the sun.

'Do you know what I felt when I found you and Gloria in here, Felix?' he says pointing at the summer house, his voice dangerously low. 'I'll tell you what I felt. I felt *relief*. I thought that I finally might be rid of both of you. I felt the last twenty years of my life rising up through me and exploding into the night. All the melodrama, the falseness, the stomach-churning anxiety I didn't even realise I'd been suffering seemed to burst from the top of my head. That's why I ran. That's why I felt the need to escape and get as far away from the pair of you as I could. I felt *free*. I thought it was the greatest moment of my life. My whole body was awash with release. I just wanted the two of you to disappear into the sunset together and leave me and my children behind.'

His whole body is shaking, like he's finally cutting out some deep cancer that's been eating him up from inside.

'But I was a fool, wasn't I? I was stupid enough to think you would fall for the bait. That when I set this whole plan in motion Gloria would inevitably leave me for you, and that you would have the decency to take her with you. To *finally* rid me of you both. Was it too much to ask?' He gives an ironic little laugh. 'I knew Gloria would walk into the trap. She was so weak that she would instinctively follow what she thought was in her heart. I knew how easily she would cave when another man gave her the attention she so desperately craved. I was right about her at least. But you? I couldn't rely on you to do this one simple thing, could I?'

My throat has gone bone dry and I struggle to articulate words. My whole destiny is being ripped from my grasp. 'You... you never wanted me, did you?' I croak. 'You just wanted me to take Gloria away so you could be free.'

'I wanted to be free of *both* of you. You're right that we've both been living a lie. But you know what the difference between us is, Felix? *My truth never involved you.*'

'No,' I say quietly. 'No, you'll change your mind. I know you will. Just give it a chance, Nevin. Give me a chance and you will see that we can have everything we've always wanted.'

'I have everything I want right now, Felix. At least, I will have when I watch your back disappear down the end of my lane.'

'NO!' I scream, rushing at him. He throws his hands up in shock as I wrap my arms around him. 'No! This wasn't how it was supposed to happen!' I envelop him in a bear hug, just wanting to hold him, to be at one with him finally, but he is struggling too much. I've come at him hard enough that we both lose our balance and topple back through the doors of the summer house.

Nevin doesn't even shout out as we fall down together, and when I land on top of him there is a sickening thud. Nevin goes still. I lie there on top of him for several seconds, not wanting to move, just to enjoy this closeness one last time before he takes it away from me. I bring my hands up to his head and pull back mine so I can look into his eyes to implore him to reconsider.

His eyes are blank, glassy. Lifeless.

'No,' I murmur as I suddenly feel wetness on my hands. Sliding them back behind his head I bring them away to see they are covered in blood. My gaze shifts to the metal crate next to his head where all the kids' outdoor sports equipment is stored. There is a large dent on its corner and a single trickle of blood running down the side.

I don't know how long I lie there on top of Nevin before a seagull cries in the distance and brings me back to reality. Then slowly I rise off him to my knees and make my way back to Coastguard's Cottage.

EPILOGUE
FELIX

So like I said, I've always wanted to live by the sea. Ever since I was little and my mother used to take me to the beach at Lyme Regis and we'd get cones of chips and ice cream with 99s for after.

A cottage by the sea, with a couple of kids running around in the garden, maybe playing with a hose, and the knowledge that I got here off my own back, not letting anything or anyone get in my way? Yeah, I guess that's what I've always secretly wanted.

A sense of belonging.

It's a shame it didn't quite work out that way.

Once I came to terms with the fact that my love was dead, and the promise of years ahead with him and his children in that little cottage by the sea was extinguished, I let my instincts kick in.

The instinct never to explain, lament or apologise.

Just to survive.

The first job was to make sure that I was never found responsible for any of the events of the past week. I scrubbed the blood from the metal crate, carefully laid Nevin on one of the yoga mats jammed in the corner, and began to drag him over the scrubland.

We didn't have far to go.

When we got to the edge of the cliff I propped him up and we sat, my arm around him, just like lovers looking out over the ocean. I felt a curious sense of déjà vu. Maybe it was because I had imagined this moment so many times over the years. Of course, Nevin was always alive when I had, and he would in turn place his arm around me and we'd sit and marvel at the view, knowing we had all we had ever wanted right there in that sunset.

As the waves broke over the rocks below, I turned and gazed at him one more time.

So close. So tender a moment.

I checked his pockets looking for his wallet and his phone, but they were empty. No surprise, he would have left them in the kitchen after we finally got the kids to sleep and made our way out onto the deck to enjoy our whisky. It seemed like so long ago, even though it was only about ten minutes. *How quickly a life can change,* I thought, and pushed him over the edge.

He fell straight down to the rocks below and the wind absorbed the thud barely a second later.

I, of course, explained to the cops how devastated he had been over the loss of his wife, and that he couldn't consider going on another day without her. They had their suspicions. That he was wracked with guilt after he murdered her and had taken the coward's way out. They even questioned me a couple more times and inferred that I had a hand in the whole sordid mess. But they couldn't prove anything. In the end they chalked it up to a tragic set of circumstances that had left a couple of kids as orphans and closed the book on the Campbells.

If Susan was devastated she hardly showed it. I think she

was more concerned with how much her life was going to change now she was responsible for bringing up Amy and Josh. She virtually cried with relief when I said I would stay in Treme and move into Coastguard's Cottage, and assume that responsibility as my own. I was Nevin's best friend after all, and it was the very least I could do. The children were all that mattered, I said. She even said she would help out financially wherever she could, and of course I modestly accepted.

For a few weeks, life was glorious. I never imagined how well I would take to parenthood. Amy and Josh were crushed at first, and Nevin's funeral was very difficult, but it's amazing how adaptable young children are. Within a week we had worked out a nice little routine and they just went on with their job of being kids. It was hard for me at first. They have the look of their father. But I always knew that would take some getting used to. I would sit on the deck at night with a whisky after they had gone to bed and just soak in the sea view across the garden.

Then came the inquest. When someone dies in mysterious circumstances the file can't be closed until the coroner has had their say. Inquiries are made, post-mortem examinations carried out and witness statements taken.

This didn't worry me particularly at first. Not until the independent judicial officers started their searches. It wasn't just Nevin's death they were investigating after all. There was the small matter of Gloria's and Derek's disappearance, and the role that Nevin may have played in that. But even then I knew that if I just stuck to the same story then the only logical outcome was a verdict of suicide for Nevin.

As Julius Caesar said, 'It's only hubris if I fail.' I had covered my tracks too well for there to be any DNA evidence, and Nevin's head injuries were consistent with a high fall onto sharp rocks. There was no incriminating CCTV footage as we've already established. I even waved the officers off as they left with Nevin's financial records, his diary and his social media logins.

All conveniently stored right there on his home computer.

And that's how Nevin had the final say. They found a Word document nestled in amongst his writings that confessed the whole shebang from the moment he approached me about initiating an affair with Gloria, to the moment we covered her and Derek with tonnes of liquid concrete. And that's when the real searches began.

At my trial I refused to give evidence and the press lapped it up. The story of a former society playboy who had conspired with his best friend to do away with the wife. Netflix are making a series about it called *The Writer, His Wife and The Concrete Killer*.

The irony of it was that I was never found responsible for Nevin's death. That was eventually ruled a suicide. No, I got forty years for murdering a woman who died because of a coffee-related accident. Oh, and Derek, so I suppose there was some justice done for his family at least.

The only thing that really got me was discovering that Gloria was pregnant. Nevin knew all along and he didn't tell me. So I suppose not only did he have the final say, but the last laugh as well.

And so yes, there is something magical about living next to the sea.

As I tilt my face into the evening breeze I can almost sense it now. The salty tang of the air. The sound of kids splashing in the water. Maybe a carousel tune floating on the breeze. I know that's absurd, given that I'm unlikely ever to see the sea again. But I believe in the power of desire, and if you desire something enough even the imagined presence of it is enough to sustain you.

A set of keys jingle behind me, and I know that's my lot for today.

'Time's up, Van Arnhem, back to your cell.'

I inhale one last time hoping to catch a wistful breath of the ocean. Then I reach my hands through the hole in the wire mesh of the exercise-yard fence, and the cuffs close around my wrists.

THE END

ACKNOWLEDGEMENTS

Enormous gratitude to the whole team at Bloodhound Books for realising my publishing dream. To my brother Tom and sister-in-law Alice for always lending an ear (and a curry). To my mum and dad since I assume my writing obsession is genetic. To friends, teachers and work colleagues around the world for inspiring these characters. And to Bo and Jimmy for giving me a reason.

ABOUT THE AUTHOR

NJ Cracknell was born in Northern Ireland during The Troubles and moved to England in his teens. He has been a music journalist, a middle manager and a voice actor, but writing is his first love. He lives in Devon as close as possible to the sea and his children.

A NOTE FROM THE PUBLISHER

Thank you for reading this book. If you enjoyed it please do consider leaving a review on Amazon to help others find it too.

We hate typos. All of our books have been rigorously edited and proofread, but sometimes mistakes do slip through. If you have spotted a typo, please do let us know and we can get it amended within hours.

info@bloodhoundbooks.com